I0587123

GOLDEN'S
RULE

GOLDEN'S RULE

A Novel

C. E. EDMONSON

TRUSTED
BOOKS
A DIVISION OF DEEP RIVER BOOKS

© 2010 by C. E. Edmonson. All rights reserved.
3rd Printing 2014

Trusted Books is an imprint of Deep River Books. The views expressed
or implied in this work are those of the author. To learn more about
Deep River Books, go online to www.DeepRiverBooks.com.

No part of this publication may be reproduced, stored in a retrieval
system, or transmitted in any way by any means—electronic, mechanical,
photocopy, recording, or otherwise—without the prior permission of
the copyright holder, except as provided by USA copyright law.

Unless otherwise noted, all Scriptures are taken from the *King James
Version* of the Bible.

ISBN 13: 978-1-63269-045-6
Library of Congress Catalog Card Number: 2009901011

For my daughters,
Chelsea & Christa

CONTENTS

OUT OF THE GAME

COACH STOVER'S FACE was as red as the *Slimshine Urgent!* lipstick that she wouldn't let me wear on the court. Intense? Major. And believe me, red was not her most flattering shade.

I mean, gimme a break. It wasn't like we were playing in the WNBA finals, or even the Olympics, which was my goal five years down the line. No, this was girls' basketball in suburban Montclair: Franklin D. Roosevelt Middle School against Benton Middle School. There were maybe thirty people in the stands, and they were barely paying attention. Plus, we were winning, 28–14, and there were only four minutes left in the game. We couldn't lose, right?

But Coach Stover was going on and on. This was our chance. Don't let up. Stay aggressive on defense. Wait for the open shot. As she ranted, she kept jabbing her finger into the playbook. Bang, bang, bang. Mouth going a mile a minute.

I looked up into the stands, but not for my folks. I had gotten beyond that disappointment long ago. Both my parents were lawyers, and they were both at their jobs. My mom was in Manhattan, some thirty miles away. She worked for the New York State Department of Finance, where she was deputy director of the trial division. My father worked for Citibank, in their international finance division. He was in Athens, Greece, toiling away on some kind of negotiations involving olive oil. I guess it was a pretty slippery deal.

But two of my friends were in the stands watching the game, a girl and a boy from my group. We called ourselves the Magnificent Seven, or the Mag-7s for short. And while we weren't exactly Alphas, we weren't losers beyond repair. But contempt for the pecking order was our thing, anyway. We lived by the motto, "Individuality or death." A bit on the dramatic side, true, but we were in eighth grade and it sounded pretty good at the time.

The Bengali Rose, Jasmine Shekhar, saw me looking up and waved. Jasmine was the Mag-7s' drama queen and a freak for vintage clothing. She spent at least one day every weekend with her older sister, Indira, wandering from thrift shop to thrift shop on the Lower East Side of Manhattan, which they considered their stomping grounds. Most kids in our class still weren't allowed to cross the Hudson River under any circumstances without their parents, except maybe for a supervised class trip.

Next to her, Ken the Karate Kid looked up when he saw Jasmine wave. He appeared confused for a moment, like he usually did. Then he lifted his hand and grinned. Kenneth Herzog was born with one leg slightly longer than the other. Even with a built-up shoe, he had a slight limp. But his parents were great compensators. They enrolled him in martial arts classes when he was seven, and now he had a second-degree black belt.

Bottom line? It was great for us. The Mag-7s were never bullied. Not even by the toughie wannabes.

"Maddie? Are you with us?"

Oops. That's me, Madison Bergamo. I smiled an of-course-I'm-listening smile. "Yes, Coach?"

"Why don't you describe the play I just called?"

This was a totally easy question. I mean, Coach Stover called the same play during every timeout. And she got just as crazy when she called it. I remember when I first made the team, how Coach gave us a little speech about everybody getting a chance to play, and being a good sport, and it was only a game, and blah, blah, blah.

Meanwhile, we lost exactly one game the whole season and Coach Stover acted like we were responsible for global warming and international terrorism, with maybe world hunger thrown in. After the game, she wouldn't even talk to us.

But when you're a kid, you're a kid. You don't have any control over the adults who run your life. If you got a psycho for a sixth grade teacher, like Mrs. Czernowitz, you just had to adapt. Same with Coach Stover. I was graduating from middle school that year. She would be at FDR forever. The thought didn't exactly make me sad. *Sayonara, Coach.*

"Cynthia brings the ball down court, then passes to me. I take the ball to the weak side. If I'm double-teamed, I find the open girl. If not, I take my defender down low."

Like I said, the same play every time. But I guess I made Coach happy because she clapped me on the back as the warning buzzer belched and the referee blew the whistle.

"Let's do this for Montclair," she said.

That's Montclair, New Jersey, right? We should do it for the town? Meanwhile, our opponent, Benton Middle School, was also located in Montclair. So winning would be as much against Montclair as for it. But who was I to argue with the coach's logic? I took the ball out, passed it to Cynthia, and trailed her down the court. When we crossed the half-court line, Cynthia flipped the ball back.

Benton's tallest player came out to meet me. She wore number 22 on her lime green uniform (much cooler than our tired out magenta togs) and she was maybe five-five. I was five-ten, not only the tallest girl but the tallest kid of either gender in the entire FDR Middle School—and that included a couple of teachers, too. Mostly, this was a source of embarrassment, as you might expect. I mean, gawky? Major. There were times I wanted to walk on my knees.

But not on a basketball court. Not only was I taller than my defender, I was faster, too—Maddie the Montclair Flash. I smiled at number 22—sneered is more like it—then cut to the left, dribbled twice and—

Fell flat on my face. That's right. *Ka-bam!*

A second later, both teams were headed back in the other direction. I tried to get up, but I couldn't get my right leg to work. I mean my leg didn't hurt or anything. In fact, it felt entirely normal. Except it wouldn't do what I told it to. My mind was going, "C'mon, leg, get it together." And my leg was going, "I can't hearrrrrrrrrr you." Now I know

4

how my mom feels when she's telling me to clean my room and I'm turning my iPod up louder.

The referee blew the whistle at that point, and Coach Stover ran across the court. She yanked down my kneepad and started squeezing my knee and my ankle. "Does this hurt? Does this?"

But there wasn't any pain. My leg wasn't even numb, like when you sit with your leg tucked under you for too long. No, what I mostly felt was embarrassed. I mean, omigosh, I'm the star of the team and I can't even stand on my own two feet. *Puh-leeeze.* I just sat there on the floor—I mean, where was I going to go?—and slowly died of embarrassment while waiting for the leg thing to pass. But it didn't.

That's when Coach Stover made it ten times worse. She told Cynthia to get the wheelchair from under the stands, and I was wheeled down a corridor that seemed about ten miles long. All the way to the nurse's room on the other side of the school. Past the lockers, the lunchroom, and the library. Fortunately, this was after classes were over and the only kids still at school were geeks from the physics club. But still, word would get out. The invincible Maddie laid low by some stupid sports injury.

Talk about a hellooooooo moment. I mean, I had good grades and everything. But so what? Ninety-five percent of FDR's students went on to college. Everybody had good grades. This was Montclair, New Jersey, where the average family in our community was considered upper middle-class. No, grades wouldn't cut it for a five-foot-ten-inch girl in eighth grade. Basketball was my thing. I was hoping to parlay my skills into a scholarship some day, and my height was going to work to my advantage for once. I mean, the wheelchair didn't even fit me, and I had to pull up my bad leg or it would've scraped the floor. I felt like a snail in a transparent shell. There was nowhere to hide—but that didn't stop me from trying my best to hide how freaked out I was feeling inside.

Nurse Cole was a tiny woman. Her shoulders were so pointy that she looked as if she forgot to take her uniform off the hanger when she put it on in the morning. She had little round eyes and her mouth was a lipless slash that turned down at the corners. Trust me on this: Nurse Cole didn't like kids. When I came through the door in that wheelchair, she put her hands on her hips and shook her head in disgust. She was packing a thermos and a plastic container in a tote bag, ready to go home now that the basketball game was almost over.

"My, my," she said, "what have we here?"

Like I was an insect that had crawled out from under the baseboards.

"Maddie Bergamo," I answered. I was using my polite voice, the one that says, I don't like you any more than you like me, but I'm being civil so there's nothing you can do about it.

"And would you mind telling me what happened to you?"

"I fell."

"Can you stand up?"

"Uh-uh. Like, my right leg isn't working."

Nurse Cole's angry glare vanished and her eyes beat a hasty retreat. Okay, *that* made me nervous. It seemed to me that in Nurse Cole's opinion, most kids who came to her office were slackers who just wanted to get out of school early. Her job was to send them back to class. But she wasn't thinking that way now.

"Are you in pain?"

"No. I just can't move it."

"And this just happened? Out of nowhere? You didn't feel any weakness before today?" She was shooting questions at me like I shoot lay-ups at practice.

"Yes, yes, and no." I wasn't trying for snotty, but I don't think I succeeded. Talk about a reality check. The truth was that I'd been perfectly fine until the moment my leg stopped working. And all of these questions weren't exactly putting my mind at ease.

"All right, up on the table." Nurse Cole helped me out of the wheelchair and onto an examining table, the kind with the roll of paper on one end. Not exactly chic *or* comfortable. Then she did exactly what Coach Stover did. She pressed my calf and my thigh, rotated my ankle, bent my knee, and rolled my hip. Everything worked fine and I could feel what she was doing, but my leg was a dead weight.

But Nurse Cole wasn't finished. She took my temperature and checked my blood pressure. She shined a light into my eyes and had me follow her finger as she waved it back and forth. Finally, she asked me a series of questions: name the school principal, the day of the week, the month of the year. Although I couldn't see how any of it was related to my leg, I played along.

"Tuttleman, Tuesday, and March," I answered without hesitation, which I guess was reassuring, because at least she didn't summon the paramedics. Good thing I don't freeze on pop quizzes.

"I'll have to call one of your parents to pick you up," she finally said.

"My mom's at work, and my dad's in Greece."

Nurse Cole's lips curled and turned into an exasperated frown. I was annoying her, which I figured was a good sign. She was back to her normal, kid-hating self.

"I didn't ask that, Maddie. But never mind. Your mother's work number will be on file in the principal's office and I'll need to consult with him anyway. Make sure you don't go anywhere."

As if I was going to get up and sprint out the door.

Only that's exactly what I wanted to do. I was one of those latchkey children who learn to take care of themselves. I know it's not fashionable—the school's Alphas would laugh in my face—but I took a lot of pride in being responsible. I picked up after myself, and I'd become a halfway decent cook. Most nights, when we didn't order in, I made dinner. In fact, I planned to put cooking on my résumé when I applied to college. Just in case basketball, and good grades, and a killer SAT score weren't enough. So, helpless-child-who-can't-stand-on-her-own-two-feet was not part of my self-image. Ken the Karate Kid might be proud of the way he overcame his disability, but my dream was a basketball scholarship. I needed to run. And for that, I needed my leg to wake up.

Thankfully, the Bengali Rose showed up for support a few minutes after Nurse Cole left for the principal's office. She asked if I was all right, but when I described what was happening to me, she changed the subject to a scarf she'd picked up for "next to nothing" over the weekend. That was her idea of a diversion tactic to get my mind off my leg. True, I was looking for something to distract me from my lifeless limb, but did it have to be something so hideous?

The scarf didn't have a label and it was major-league ugly—small purple and black checks with scarlet fringes—but she was sure it was a *Hermes*.

"I practically stole it," she announced.

"Congratulations," I answered, stopping short of asking if she could break back into the scene of the crime and return it to the bargain bin where it belongs. "Do you mind telling me who won the game?"

"We did, but it was close. The team kinda fell apart when you…when you left."

The Bengali Rose was a short, pretty girl with big black eyes, a pouty mouth, a pointy little chin…and obviously a *huge* phobia of nurses' offices. She looked more bugged out about being there than I was.

And to tell you the truth, she was dressed more for an art gallery opening than she was for Nurse Cole's office. She was wearing a long blue sweater that fell to her hips, a patterned skirt that dropped to her ankles, and button-up shoes that must have been like a hundred years old. Bizarre, to say the least. But there was plenty of room for girls like Jasmine in Montclair. The town was an ethnic potpourri, with about one-third of its residents African-American, more than half Caucasian, and the rest Asian, Latino, East Indian, and other. Jasmine fit right in.

Come to think of it, I did, too. My mother is black and my father is white, but only once did I have any trouble.

That was back in fourth grade when some of the black kids started calling me Oreo, like the cookie: black on the outside, white on the inside. At first, I was devastated. I mean, I was only ten. My psyche was fragile. But then I decided that I was what I was, and I better get used to it. With my mom's help, I had a t-shirt made up and wore it to school once a week for the rest of the year:

**PROUD TO BE
MULTIRACIAL**

"So," Jasmine said, looking for another way to change the subject, "what's up with Jason Walker?"

I frowned. Well, that did it. She definitely got my mind on something else! Like a bum leg wasn't bad enough.

I'd had a major crush on Jason going back to the beginning of seventh grade, but I couldn't seem to catch his attention. That's most likely because I was six inches taller than he was. But I mean, he'd eventually catch up, right? Girls mature earlier, so what's the big deal? I even arranged to get partnered with him in science lab. He was nice and all, but he totally did not see me that way, *if* he saw me at all. Who knows? Maybe he never looked up. Outside of the experiment, the only thing he ever talked about was competing with his friends at Xbox video games, especially his favorites: *Grand Theft Auto* and *Halo 2*.

Okay, so he still had a few years to go before he was really eligible. And if he didn't have those sapphire blue eyes, I wouldn't have noticed him in the first place, either. But FDR's spring dance was coming up in a few weeks and I'd invested too much time in Jason to find someone else now.

The funny part was that I didn't really want to go to the dance at all. Not many of us did. In fact, nobody ever, like, actually *danced*. The dance was like so retro and we were way too cool. I mean, what'd we do to deserve this? But if nobody asked me, I wouldn't have a chance to say no. It would be more like the dance was rejecting *me*. Plus, it seemed like most of the other girls already had dates.

"I tell you," I told Jasmine, "if Jason doesn't mature soon, I'm gonna have to ask Ken."

"Forget the Karate Kid. He says he's not goin'."

"Even better."

Jasmine was about to respond when my right leg, the one I couldn't move, suddenly twitched. At first, I was like, "Now what?" Then a minute later, my leg was back to normal. I mean one hundred percent completely normal, like nothing had ever happened.

First thing, I stood up and walked around the room. In fact, I was practically skipping when Nurse Cole bustled through the door. That was another thing about Nurse Cole. She was a great bustler. Even when she had nothing to do, she was straightening up or checking her supplies. Still, this time she stopped in her tracks, mouth open.

"What happened?"

"I got better." To prove my point, I launched into a jumping jack. Pretty impressive, right? "I'm ready to go home."

One look into Nurse Cole's beady little eyes put that hope to rest. I wasn't going anywhere. Stupid school rules. It was nothing, a muscle spasm, at most. Even pro athletes got them from pushing too hard.

That's what I told *myself* anyway. All I said to Nurse Cole was, "Can I at least go to my locker and change? I haven't even taken a shower." This was true—my hair was a sweaty, sticky mess—and I wrestled with my tangled scrunchie as Nurse Cole shook her head.

"I've spoken to Principal Tuttleman," she announced as though she'd just had an audience with the Pope. Or maybe the Wizard of Oz. "You're to remain here until your mother arrives to take you home."

Nurse Cole pulled herself up to her full height, which was all of about five feet, and squeezed her jaw shut. I had to halfway beg her to let Jasmine get my clothes so I could change in the office. Then I got to sit for the next hour and a half before my mom arrived.

During that time, I was caught somewhere between thrilled beyond belief that my leg was fine, hoping really hard that it would stay that way, and worried about what would happen when my mom realized that we dragged her down here for nothing. But mostly I was bored. Even the novelty of swinging *both* my legs out from under my chair was beginning to wear thin after awhile. I couldn't wait for Mom to get here soon and spring me loose. Otherwise, I was considering making a run for it, now that I was able to.

My friends have a nickname for my mom, Abigail Moore-Bergamo. They call her *Type A*. That's because she's always running around organizing every little aspect of her life. In her work, that's a pretty good thing. I've seen her in action on take-your-kid-to-work day. In a courtroom, she generally gets what she wants, with juries and judges alike—not to mention at home. Forceful is the best description. Whatever Abigail needs or desires, Abigail gets. According to my grandmother, she was always like that.

So, like, naturally, when Mom arrived, she started right in on Nurse Cole. I swear, it was like the irresistible force meeting the immovable object. While Mom hit her with question after question, Nurse Cole folded her arms across her chest and tightened her thin little mouth until it almost disappeared. All the while, I was hopping around the room like the Easter Bunny. *Hey, check me out, I'm a hundred percent recovered. Take a look, please.*

But nobody was paying any attention to me. Jasmine had left (although I wished she could have witnessed this), and my mom and Nurse Cole were locked in mortal combat.

"I'm not a physician, Mrs. Bergamo…"

"Moore-Bergamo," Mom automatically corrected.

Nurse Cole's smile was as cold as ice. "I'm not a physician, Mrs. Moore-Bergamo, but I can tell you this: loss of function in a limb can be a serious symptom. Maddie must see a doctor and I cannot allow her to return to school, much less engage in sports, without a physician's note pronouncing her fit."

Mom tried to get Nurse Cole to name a few of those causes—and I was kind of curious, too—but like I said, Nurse Cole was playing the part of immovable object. She wasn't a doctor and she wasn't about to diagnose an unknown disorder and if Mom didn't like it, maybe she could try home schooling. I was sitting there silently like, what's there to argue about? It was weird; it happened once. Let's build a bridge and get over it, people.

Mom stood her ground for a few minutes longer, then caved in.

And I mean, what choice did she have? At Franklin D. Roosevelt Middle School, when it came to matters of health, Nurse Cole's word was law.

Chapter 2

THE JOURNEY BEGINS

MOM WAS ON the phone the minute we walked through the door. She was calling Dr. Martin, my pediatrician (yes, I was still seeing a pediatrician—talk about mortifying) to arrange an appointment. The office was closed, naturally, and she got his answering service. I didn't listen to the conversation, but I'm pretty certain she used her I'm-a-lawyer-and-don't-mess-with-me line, because she always did. Unfortunately, the attack failed, just like with Nurse Cole. My mom was told to take me to the emergency room if I needed immediate care. Otherwise, she could phone Dr. Martin in the morning.

While this was going on, I was in the kitchen, emptying the dishwasher. Talk about feeling guilty. I mean, *puh-leeeze.* Emergency care? A one-time sports injury was hardly an emergency, and I liked to think that I was beyond needing care. Daycare, childcare, even caring much about the dance—all in the past.

Independence was my thing. I took care of myself. Not that I was a drudge; I didn't mop the floor or clean the bathroom. We had a housekeeper who came in twice a week, on Monday and Thursday. But I did make my bed, and pick up after myself, and do the occasional laundry. Now my mom would have to take a day off; maybe more than one. I mean, who knew where this was going? And all this drama over something that had already magically healed itself! If only my leg could write a medical note.

After she gave up on bullying the answering service, Mom ordered up a thin-crust pizza and a Greek salad and we sat down to a mostly silent dinner. I could see that she was more worried than she let on, but there wasn't much I could do about it besides assuring her that I was fine and suggesting that I go to the doctor alone, or that we make an evening appointment. I wanted to get this ordeal over with as soon as possible and get back to normal, like my leg had already decided to do. Mom wasn't listening, though. It seemed that Nurse Cole's nervousness was infectious.

"Don't worry," she told me over nibbles of mushroom pizza. "Come tomorrow morning, I'll get us an early appointment. I promise you."

I *wasn't* worried. But the more the adults acted serious and strange, the more worried I was becoming.

I went up to my room after dinner and sent a collective text message to the Mag-7s, just in case they hadn't heard from Jasmine. The responses poured in—mostly questions I didn't have answers for. After texting back a series of "IDK" ("I don't know"), I suddenly discovered that my "attack" was something I didn't want to talk about. It's like when

I'm on the basketball court and I'm knocking down shot after shot. You don't want to jinx yourself by talking about the streak. So, I made an excuse about having homework to do and signed off.

I guess I was expecting NBDs ("no big deal") instead of this outpouring of concern. People break their legs or tear muscles on the court all the time. That was something we had all seen up close and personal—and let me tell you, it isn't pretty. Really, my leg spazzing out was no big deal in comparison. So why were the kids all of a sudden acting as crazy as the adults?

So, I did what I told them I was going to do and actually *attempted* to get some homework done—but I couldn't concentrate on the math problems in my workbook. See! I told you the craziness was catching! I finally found myself staring at the photos on the wall opposite the foot of my bed: my Wall of Fame.

President Barack Obama was there, along with singer Alicia Keys, baseball great Derek Jeter, musician Lenny Kravitz, and two of my favorite actresses, Tia and Tamara Mowry. There were dozens of other photos as well, including the author Walter Mosley, and news correspondents Soledad O'Brien and Christiane Amanpour. These were some of my favorites as well, role models for my writer ambitions. Especially Soledad and Christiane, fearless reporters who'd been covering news stories around the world for the past twenty years.

But that wasn't why they were up there. No, everybody on my Wall of Fame was multiracial. And my PROUD TO BE MULTIRACIAL t-shirt, long since outgrown, was tacked right in the middle of the photos.

This was another piece of my personal puzzle. Like being independent, defiance was a shield. Montclair was like this integrated oasis. Yeah, we had our gangsta wannabes, rocker wannabes, jock wannabes, and preppy wannabes, too. But wannabes or not, we had one thing in common. We'd been prepped for success, like from the day we were born. So it wasn't a question of whether or not we'd go to college. The issue was whether we'd get into a top-tier university like Duke or Stanford, or one of the Ivy League schools, or the big burrito in the sky, MIT.

And my *new* question was whether I'd get there on a basketball scholarship or not. Because if something serious was really happening with my leg…I stopped myself from completing the thought. I really didn't want to jinx myself. It was just that everyone's sympathy was starting to spook me out.

Eventually, I settled down. I actually did a few of the math problems and read a chapter in my history book about Prohibition before I went to sleep. Like, normal, okay? That's what I wanted. It was scary while it lasted but now it was over—all except getting a doctor's note. A pure technicality. Students came to school with those things all the time, waving them in the air like they were get-out-of-gym-free cards. And there was never anything wrong with any of those kids.

I told myself it was time to get back to worrying about more important issues, like a date for the spring dance, and should I go to basketball camp or try to catch on with a local summer league, and isn't it about time I buckled down because mid-term exams were coming up in a few weeks and I hadn't so much as looked at George Orwell's

Animal Farm? And somewhere in the midst of all of that, I managed to fall asleep.

The next morning, I swung my legs over the side of the bed and stood up. Nothing out of whack. Totally cool. It was a minor glitch, that's all. I was ready to get my doctor's note and move on.

I brushed my teeth and took a shower, then dressed and went into the kitchen. Mom was pouring some kind of granola into a bowl and there was a glass of juice next to my place at the breakfast bar. I sat down, picked up the juice, brought it to my lips and—

Passed out cold. *Thwack!*

I woke up totally confused. The only thing I knew, from the *omigosh* expression on Mom's face, was that something really bad had happened to me. My brain was spinning like a top and I had to wait for it to slow down before I was finally able to sit up. Then I tested my arms and legs, one at a time. Everything worked.

"Mom, what happened?"

"I think you had a seizure."

"What?" I heard the words, but it was like I couldn't understand them. Not when they were being spoken about *me*.

My mom took me in her arms and lifted me to my feet. She led me, stumbling, into the living room, then onto the couch.

"I'm going to call Dr. Martin right now."

When my mom left the room, it was the first time I became seriously scared. A bum leg was one thing. But blackouts and seizures? Maybe Nurse Cole wasn't just being an unreasonable dictator by making me go see a doctor. Maybe something *really was* wrong with me… *horribly* wrong.

I counted the seconds until my mom came back into the room. One hundred and twenty-three. Alone like that, helpless, not knowing what was happening to me, they were the longest two minutes of my life.

Before I knew it, my mother and I were on our way to the emergency room at the Essex County Medical Center, following Dr. Martin's recommendation. I mean, given a choice, I would have gladly gone to the pediatrician instead of the ER. Emergency rooms are for really bad cases, like car crash victims or someone with an axe stuck in his head or people who accidentally cut off their fingers while chopping up carrots with a kitchen knife (something my mom always warned me about). The only other time I was rushed to an ER before was when I was little and stuck loose beads from my Barbie bracelet way up my nose and couldn't get them out. Life or death stuff. Like, actual *emergencies*. Not like now. Right?

I wanted to ask my mom, but didn't. Instead, I fiddled with the radio and watched cars zip by in the other direction as I tried to fight off one of those Chicken-Little-was-right moments. I mean, word up, the sky *was* falling. Seizures? I was fourteen and this absolutely could not be happening to me.

I glanced at my mother from time to time but avoided making real eye contact. I couldn't stand to see the worry in her eyes. Knowing that she was scared would have made the situation so much worse. So I just focused on her voice, soothingly repeating, "It's okay, baby. We'll be there soon.

Everything will be okay." I think she was trying to convince herself as much as me.

They took us seriously in the emergency room. I mean the triage nurse, and the examining nurse, and Dr. Sandoval when she came into my little cubicle. In fact, they let us in almost right away, before the grayish-looking guy with the hacking cough and the woman with a dishtowel tied around her arm as a makeshift tourniquet, both of whom had been there ahead of us. I wouldn't have minded waiting. Really. That was one race I actually *didn't* want to win.

Dr. Sandoval was a heavyset woman, in her thirties, wearing pink scrubs. She conducted almost the same examination Nurse Cole had on the prior afternoon—except this time around, I think I forgot to breathe once during the entire thing.

"I don't find any gross abnormalities," she told my mother afterward, much to my relief. "Still, I'd like to order a CT scan of Madison's brain."

A scan? Of *my brain?* What?! Had something gone wrong with my hearing now, too?

"I'd order an MRI, but your insurance company won't approve the test," Dr. Sandoval continued matter-of-factly.

"The insurance company?" Mom asked. "Tell me why."

"They feel we should do the CT scan first. And fighting them will only cause a delay."

Finally, I couldn't stand it any longer. I was pretty sure the doctor just said "brain scan" and now these people were chatting about insurance? "Helloooooooo? Maddie calling. Do you wanna tell me what's wrong with my brain, or is it a secret?"

Dr. Sandoval and my mom both looked at me as if they'd forgotten I was there. Like I was something they'd misplaced. Then Mom reached down to stroke my hair. "Sorry, baby," she said.

We were inside a narrow space separated from similar spaces on either side by curtains. I was lying on one of those rolling hospital beds, called gurneys, mainly because there was nowhere else to sit or lie down. My mom was forced to stand up, and with Dr. Sandoval in the space, it was like we were jammed into a closet.

Dr. Sandoval turned to me. Like everybody in the emergency room—the nurses, the doctors, the aides, and even the patients—she looked as if she needed to be somewhere else in a big hurry. But she forced herself to focus on me for the time being—and the expression on her face made me wish she hadn't. It looked like she was trying to screw up the courage to tell me something, and I realized that it would have been easier to let her just keep talking over me instead of *to* me directly. That way, we could have both pretended she was talking about someone else.

"The purpose of the CT scan is to determine what, if anything, is wrong with you," she said. "But it's possible that you've had a mild stroke."

Mild? Gimme a break! That's how I order my General Tsao's chicken. But a fourteen-year-old kid with a stroke? There's nothing mild about that, any way you look at it. This is, like, guess what? Somebody tossed a refrigerator out of a window and it landed on your head. But don't worry. It was empty.

"The procedure," she continued, "is simple. We'll inject contrast material through a vein and take a few pictures. Nothing to it. It's entirely painless."

Yeah, for *you*, I thought.

And then she was gone, off to give thirty seconds of her precious time to some other chump. Mom sat next to me on the gurney. Her eyes were red and swollen, and her forehead was lined with tension.

"I don't think it'll be anything," I told her. "I feel great." *Physically*, that was true.

"I know, honey. You're a strong girl," she said, squeezing my hand. "Just keep being strong." Then she stood up and paced around the small space. "I need to get in touch with your father."

"You didn't call him last night?"

"I tried, but his cell phone was out of reach. Anyway, it's probably better if we get this pinned down first."

I wanted to ask why, but a nurse pulled the curtain aside and stepped up next to the gurney. She was carrying a plastic container full of needles and vials. My eyes grew wide at the sight of them and I shot my mom a quick look of panic. I mean, she wouldn't let me rent any of the *Friday the 13th* movies because I'd have nightmares—and now I was living one!

"We'll just take a little blood," the nurse said, smiling sweetly. "Just a pinch is all."

Promises, promises, that's all I got. She had to make three attempts before she hit a vein. I mean, was she a trainee? Or did she just like to torture people? Not that she was apologetic or anything. No, her failures didn't seem to bother her very much—she somehow kept up that beauty pageant smile, like someone was going to hand her a crown and a bunch of roses after this. With any luck, they'd have thorns on them.

Hey, I was allowed to be bitter about this. After all, it was my arm getting stuck like a voodoo doll—I halfway expected to look down and see the nurse's initials tattooed on it.

When she finally finished taking the blood and labeling the vials, she handed me a plastic container with a lid and directed me to the bathroom. "We'll need a urine sample, too. Drop it off at the nurses' station when you're finished," she said cheerily.

Then she was gone, no doubt off to find her next victim. And I was, like, so totally bummed out I couldn't even talk. I felt like I was disappearing, the incredible shrinking Maddie—like I wasn't a person anymore, just a series of test results or a lab rat to be tormented and studied.

"Do you want me to go to the bathroom with you?" my mom asked.

Oh, yeah, like that'd make it better.

I did my duty, then settled back on the gurney to wait, wishing I'd thought to bring a book or something. Anything to take my mind off of what was going on around me, to me...*inside* of me. It seemed surreal to be sitting there while everyone else went about their usual business, poking and prodding patients, and talking about strokes like they were the most normal things in the world.

I guess if you work in a hospital, that kind of stuff becomes second nature to you. But to me, it was as if my life had been turned upside down in just a matter of a few hours. Nothing was *less* normal than sitting here on the gurney, waiting to find out what was wrong with me. Being probed by aliens wouldn't have been much weirder!

But everything *was* normal just yesterday morning, just a short twenty-four hours ago. Life was perfect. No complaints. Now here I was, being checked for signs of a stroke. Could this *really* be happening to me? I kept wanting to wake up or turn back time. With something this serious, shouldn't they give you at least one do-over?

My answer arrived in the form of an aide pushing a wheelchair. I *did* get a do-over—unfortunately, with the wheelchair! Why did I need one when I could walk? Hospital rules.

My mom and I looked at each other, but I think we both knew that we couldn't fight procedure. Better to get it over with. I sat down with a sigh. Only the trip was even more depressing than lying on the gurney. When you're in a wheelchair in a hospital, everybody looks at you. Like, what's wrong with *this one?* And the elevator they put me on was already occupied by an old man on a gurney who stared at the ceiling and groaned with every breath. I don't even think he was in pain or anything. He was just groaning. Maybe that was his way of protesting against what was happening to him.

I understood how he felt. I wanted to groan myself.

In the CT room, some space-age-looking equipment was set up, similar to what I saw on the school trip to the planetarium. I focused on that while another nurse pushed an IV into the same vein used to take blood. "Just a little pinch, dear." Then before I knew what was happening to me, I was put on a platform that slid into a machine that completely encircled my head. "Don't move, dear." A liquid was injected into my arm and the machine began to spin, whirring like the sound of birds' wings, first to the left, then back to the right, finally making a sound that reminded me of bees in a hive.

Being in there was one of the worst experiences of my life. I felt so utterly alone, so cut off from everyone in the outside world. Almost like a living robot. And it didn't take just a minute, like X-rays in a dentist's office. By the time the machine stopped, I felt like I was the victim of a cave-in. Don't move? It was all I could do not to jump off the table and run away from the machine that was trying to devour me headfirst.

I was feeling dizzy when I finally got to my feet, but the unit was already being prepared for the next patient. My mother was arguing with the X-ray technician, who wanted us to go back to the emergency room. The scans, she told him, would have to be read in this very unit by a radiologist, so returning to the emergency room was pointless. Therefore, we'd be sitting in the small waiting area until that radiologist made an appearance. Then she handed him her business card: Abigail Moore-Bergamo, Attorney at Law.

"Hospitals," she told the man, "have certain obligations with regard to their patients, obligations that are best honored. We'll be in the waiting area." It was a small victory but, as Coach Stover taught me, every win counts.

I held my tongue until we were sitting next to each other on plastic chairs, the kind with a little depression that never really fits your bottom. "What kind of obligations do hospitals have?" I asked. The question was sincere. I mean, I couldn't demand my rights if I didn't know what they were, right? But Mom was a step ahead of me.

"I have no idea, but at least he didn't call security," she said, and we both started laughing. For me, the laughter was a kind of release of all my pent-up nerves. For Mom, the laughter turned into tears that suddenly streamed down her face. Finally, she swiped at her eyes. "Don't you worry, baby. Whatever happens, we'll get through it together."

Okay, so it's just what you'd tell a little kid, which a day before I definitely didn't want to be. But it worked. I felt better—at least until Dr. Rosenberg came into the waiting area holding a sheet of X-ray film. Then my nerves began to act up again. It was worse than getting back results for a test you weren't prepared for.

Dr. Rosenberg was a younger man, most likely still in his twenties. Like Dr. Sandoval, his eyes were red, his eyelids swollen. He looked as though he hadn't slept in a week. Still, he did manage to smile as he introduced himself.

"Would you like to discuss this in private?" he asked my mother.

Mom's response was quick in coming. "No," she announced as she moved over to allow him to sit between us. "We're in this together." She flashed me a brave smile.

Dr. Rosenberg sat down. "I don't want to sugarcoat what I'm about to tell you, because it's serious." He turned up the X-ray to reveal what was obviously a brain—*my* brain—and pointed to a white patch on the left side. "This disorder might be some sort of inflammation, or even multiple sclerosis." Then he paused briefly. "But the most likely cause is a brain tumor. An MRI will tell us for sure."

He went on for several minutes, but I didn't hear a word. There was a voice inside my head, screaming so loud I couldn't hear anything else. The voice's vocabulary consisted of two words: *brain* and *tumor*. And that's all I heard as we made our way out of the hospital and drove home.

Brain tumor, brain tumor, brain tumor. Can you hear me now? Can you hear me now? Brainnnnnn Tuuuuuumorrrrrrrrrrrrrr.

I felt like I was floating, like my mind had left my body and was off alone somewhere, trying to escape and return back to the reality that made sense to me: the girls' locker room before yesterday's game. Even history class, which I was missing right now. Anywhere but here, now, in this car, next to my mother, who was trying so hard not to cry.

I couldn't cry, either, because crying would mean that, at least emotionally, I had accepted this situation. Which I hadn't. At all. It was grotesque. Wrong. What the doctor said was a mistake. The MRI would clear it all up. It had to.

As soon as we entered the house, Mom was on the phone. Two phones, actually—the house phone and her cell phone. She was doing what she does best: taking command. I didn't blame her. Controlling the situation was the only defense she had. Abigail Moore-Bergamo would find the best doctors, and the best hospitals, and the earliest appointment for her daughter.

And me? The daughter part? I still couldn't get my mind around what was happening. Didn't Dr. Rosenberg say it might *not* be a tumor? Didn't he say something about an inflammation? Okay, so I didn't have the faintest idea what an inflammation was. But why get technical? It had to be better than a brain tumor—and it was the only hope I had.

I left Mom to her phoning, went to my room, and turned on my computer. For the next hour, I played a game of pretend. I pretended that nothing had changed and my history paper on Prohibition still needed to be written. When in doubt, Google. That's the way we all did it. Google and Wikipedia and a trip to the library for a few titles we could stick in the bibliography. I briefly thought about searching "brain tumor" and "inflammation" and even "multiple sclerosis," but I didn't. Like I said, why jinx myself? Besides, the Internet was good, but it wouldn't give me all the answers.

I printed out what I found as I went along, until my printer tray was full. Then I read through the articles until I found an angle I could work. I mean, we're talking about a middle school essay. Nobody expected scholarship. But I definitely wanted an A and figured I could get it with an organization called the Women's Christian Temperance Union, an organization devoted to outlawing alcohol. My history teacher, Ms. Marrano, was big on women's issues.

By the time I finished up, I thought I was feeling better. I thought I was strong enough to e-mail the Mag-7s. I thought I was ready to type the words *brain* and *tumor* as a remote possibility. And maybe I was, because I managed to hit the right keys and click the SEND button. In fact, I didn't realize that I was crying until I shut down the computer and the screen went dark, and I saw the tears streaming down my face.

Then I blubbered like a baby, and I kept on blubbering. Brain tumor? Brain tumor? No, that wasn't right. I was only fourteen—my life was just starting out. I was the Montclair Flash. Now you see me, now you don't. The fastest girl in the school. An athlete. Strong. Healthy. Unstoppable. Was it possible that my body would turn against me like that?

My mother came into the room before I broke down altogether. Maybe she was using some of that mom radar. Or maybe I was emitting some kind of kid-in-distress signal: beep, beep, beep. But when she took me in her arms, I didn't try to pretend that I was too old to be held. No way. I was scared out of my mind, and the safest place I could think of was right where I was then.

She cradled me, rocking slightly back and forth, stroking my hair and all the while whispering, "Ssshhh, it's okay. I won't let anything happen to you." She kept repeating that until I finally believed it.

Eventually, I calmed down enough to go into the bathroom and wash my face. After I shut off the water and toweled dry, I stared at my reflection in the mirror for just a moment. Mostly, I think I'm a cute kid. My skin is the color of coffee ice cream and, at least on this particularly day, relatively zit-free. My eyes are light brown and large enough to draw compliments from my relatives; my mouth is full and my chin firm. But I wasn't looking at my features. I was running my fingers through my hair, searching for a lump, as if brain tumors grew on the outside of the skull.

"Honey, you all right?" my mother called from the other room.

"Yeah, fine."

I took a last look—still no lump. But the face in the mirror seemed strange somehow, far away, foreign. It didn't feel like *me* anymore. I stared back at her for a few seconds, then turned out the light and headed back to my bedroom.

Mom was sitting on the edge of my bed, holding what looked like a book in her lap. It was about the size of my algebra book, covered in brown leather, and about an inch thick.

"What's that?"

"It's a memoir, honey, written by your great-great-great-grandmother. Her name was Golden Lea Jackson and she was born sometime during the 1830s. She called her memoir *Recollections*. It's about her time growing up as a slave in Kentucky, and it's been passed down to the women in the family for more than a hundred years. I've been saving it for when you're older."

The first thing I thought was, *And you're giving it to me now because I might not get older?* But Mom was having enough trouble dealing with the situation, so I kept that particular thought to myself.

"Golden who?" I said. "My great-great-great what?"

"Your great-great-great-grandmother." My mother patted the bed alongside her, and I sat down. "The book was written in Golden Lea's own hand and the ink was starting to fade, so we had the pages bound into this book with archival page sleeves to preserve them. You'll have to be careful while you're reading, because the paper is very brittle."

"Why don't you just make a photocopy of it? Or scan a digital copy?"

"We have made copies, honey, of course. But reading the words in Golden Lea's own hand is a way of reaching back to touch the past. At least, it was for me." Mom stopped long enough to put her arm around my shoulders. "I know you're looking ahead, baby, into the future. That's natural at your age. But sometimes the past can help us deal with the present. Your great-great-great-grandmother was a woman with true spirit, a fighter to her bones."

I started to shake my head. I didn't want to be tied to a black past any more than I wanted to be tied to a white past. But I couldn't say that, just like I couldn't talk about a future without me in it.

"All right, Mom," I finally said. "I'll give it a try. But I just hope it's not too depressing. I mean, I'm not trying to be a wise guy, but slavery doesn't sound all that uplifting."

Mom smiled and hugged me, then stood up to go. "I'm still trying to reach your father. I left word at his hotel, but I'm going to try calling him again."

I waited until she left the room, then opened the book. My first thought was that I was in for a tough time. The handwriting inside was very neat, but also very small, and the black ink was pretty faded and many of the letters ran together. Plus, there were no lines on the pages and the words slanted up to the right. I told myself, *You so totally don't need this right now.*

But I was wrong. I did need Golden Lea Jackson's book. I needed to step out of my own skin for a while, get outside of my own headspace. I needed to hear from someone who survived an almost impossible situation and reached out to guide future generations of her family to do the same. And I didn't have to read more than a few paragraphs before I was utterly hooked.

Chapter 3

LITTLE GIRL LOST

Recollections

MY NAME IS *Golden Lea Jackson Pitts and this here is the recollections of my life. The first thing I gotta ask is that whoever comes to read this story in the future, please forgive my writin. Mosly, I had to learn readin and writin on my own. I got pretty good at readin cause I had me a chance to practice, but I never did git much chance to practice my writin when I was a growin up on Masta Harris Jackson's plantation. I will tell how this come to pass in due time.*

Fact, when my daughter, Ophelia, asked me to set down my membrances bout growin up, I was right opposed to the idea. But Ophelia ain't nothin, if she ain't persistent. I gotta do this, she says near bout every day, so her daughter will know bout slavery times, and her daughter's daughter, too. It was a duty I had to perform for the family.

I tole her them was some mighty hard times and nobody should have to think too hard on em. But Ophelia's bout as stubborn as the day is long and she jus finally wore me out.

I was born sometime durin the late 1830s. I can't say when exactly cause nobody kep no records of when slaves was born, nor when they died. But I believe it was near 1838 cause Pa tole me that my mama was sold off the plantation when I was three years old. That's when I was given to be the personal slave of Missy Ann, who was two. Now I knowed for a fact that Missy Ann was born in 1839, so I reckon I gotta be born bout 1838.

I don't rememba nothin bout my mama. Don't rememba her bein sold off, neither. My pa, Elijah, was a stable groom, and he tole me that I was near to broke in pieces. He said I didn't speak for six months, nor barely moved, and Masta was bout to send me to live in the cabins with the other slave chirrens. Masta said I was a ungrateful child. But then I started talkin again, so I stayed in the big house.

But if I didn't rememba nothin bout Mama bein sold off, later on I did imagine how it happened. That come bout after I seen a slave trader drive his slaves up to the plantation.

The Jackson Plantation was called Belle Maison and it was located in the state of Kentucky, where it gits mighty wet and cold in the winter. So the slave traders only come in the summertime when the roads is dried up. I musta been bout four years old the first time a slave trader come to the house. I rememba I was on the porch with Missy Ann when I seen a cloud of dust bout a mile down the road. The cloud was comin closer, but very slow. Not like the Masta's carriage, or mens on horses. More like the cloud was driftin.

Masta Harris come out on the porch bout then. Jus stood there with his hands on his hips, like he figurin hard in his head. Missy Ann was nappin in the little crib she used on the porch and I was rockin her slowly, like I was sposed to. But Masta didn't pay no attention to neither one of us. Only took his hat off and wiped his head with a big ol handkerchief. Then Winnie come out carryin a tray with a pitcher of lemonade and some glasses on it, so I knowed somethin was gonna happen. Winnie was Mistriss Sarah's personal slave.

Finally, the cloud of dust gits close enough to where I can see three mens. The mens was mounted up and they was carryin pistols tucked into their waists and they had whips draped over their saddles. Their hat brims was very wide and hung down over their faces and they drooped in the saddle, like they come a far piece. A long line of what looks to me like ghosts stretched out behind em.

At first, I was right scared and I wanted to run off. But I knew if I left Missy Ann alone, I'd git my legs switched, so I jus tried to make myself small. That's when I realized them ghosts was really peoples—slaves covered with dust so thick they was near mos white. Lands, there musta been a hundred of em. Mens, womens, and chirrens. Babies, too. And ceptin for the babies, each one of em had a iron collar runnin right round their necks. A long chain run through rings on the collars and I could hear that ol chain clankin on the stones in the road as they come up the drive. The slaves was holdin the chain up so it wouldn't be draggin on their necks, but the chain was long enough to hit the ground anyway. Goin clank, clank, clank with every step they takes.

Now I ain't gonna make no big story outta this, cause that ain't what I'm after tellin. Sides, peoples mosly talk too much anyway, always makin the simplest thing go on forever. The trader's name was Marston and he was the one rode up to the porch, an older man with mustaches that dripped down past *his chin. The other two mens was his overseers and they kep a respectful distance till Masta invited them forward.*

Slaves was Marston's business. If you was in need of slaves, he'd sell em to ya. If you was after sellin slaves, he'd buy em. That particular day, Masta didn't need no slaves and didn't wanna sell none, neither. But he was right cordial. He offered Marston and his overseers lemonade and they stood there for a few minutes, chattin bout the price of tobacco, which was Masta's cash crop. Then Masta asked Marston does he want water fetched for his slaves. But Marston, he said, "No, they can jus drink outta the streams with the horses." Then Marston and his overseers started off, walkin the horses back the way they come. And the slaves started up after em. Didn't have to be tole or nothin. Jus picks up their feet and chains and follers down the road.

Not right away, but after a time thinkin it over, what I done was imagine my mama gettin sold. I imagined the slave trader and Masta Harris makin a deal, like I seen him do in later times, and my mama bein led out to the back of the line. In my mind, I see a collar fixed round her neck and a chain run through the collar and Mama standin out from the rest cause she's the only one who ain't covered with white dust. And I see her lookin back to the house as the long line begins to move. I hear her cryin out to me, her onliest child, as the dust rises to shroud her in haze.

"Good-bye, my daughter. Good-bye, my love. For I will never see you no more. Farewell, farewell."

We made or growed mos everythin we used or ate at Belle Maison. We had carpenters and a blacksmith and a little mill on the stream where we ground corn and wheat. In the fields, we growed greens, taters, snap beans, peas, corn, squashes, and bout every kinda melon there is. We had sheep for wool, which the women field hands spun in the winter. We had cattle and hogs and chickens for meat, and cows for milk and butter. We growed apples and pears in the orchard. Yessuh, we sure growed a lot of food. Only it weren't for the field hands. No, the slaves was fed thisaway. The house slaves got scraps from the table. The hands who done special work, the blacksmith and the carpenter and the stable hands, got reglar meat rations. The chirrens who was too little to work in the fields was fed cornmeal and milk. The cook mushed it up in the kitchen and carried it to the yard in buckets. Then she dumped them buckets into a trough, like you uses to feed the livestock, and them chirrens gotta run and git it right fast fore it's all gone.

The field slaves got a ration of cornmeal, molasses, peas, and greens every Sunday and had to make it last through the whole week. Only there weren't never enough, not for no man or woman who was out in the fields fore sunup and didn't come in till it was too dark to see a hand in front of their own face. Sometimes, the field slaves was able to sneak out in the middle of the night to fish in the creek, but mosly they stole food from Masta's gardens to git by. Masta didn't spend much time at Belle Maison. He was some kinda mucky-muck in Kentucky politics and he was always in Louisville or Frankfort. The plantation was run by Masta's overseer. His name was Henry Sewell and he was quick to whip any slave he caught stealin. Myself, I don't know what that man figured, cause you can beat a starvin man halfway to death and he still gonna steal food iffen he be hungry enough. But that's the way they done it. Henry Sewell was always fast to the whip if a field slave was stealin or slackin off.

Mista Henry Sewell didn't have nothin to do with the house slaves, for which I guess was our fortune. And he didn't mess much with the stable hands, long as they kep his horse fit. That was cause we raised thorobred horses on that Kentucky plantation. Them horses was Masta's pride and it was my pa who mosly took care em when they was in the barn. And they wasn't no easy horses to git along with. Fact, some of them thorobreds Masta Harris owned, they'd kick to death any man that tried to enter their stall. Ceptin for Pa. He jus had that way and the horses trusted him. He was the one groomed em and tended to their ailments.

Masta, he did have himself a vetranarian name of Doctor Manville. He was a nervous little fella, kep all his medicines in a buckboard he rode out to the farms. I rememba one time he tried to examine a horse name of Greenback. Now Greenback was ornery as all git out and he bit Doctor Manville hard in the shoulder one day. Tore out a big ol chunk of flesh. After that, Doctor Manville grew mighty careful. He reglar stood outside the stall, tellin my pa, do this and do that.

I was allowed to stay with my pa on Saturday nights. The way Pa tole it, Mistriss Sarah started lettin me go to him back when I was grievin for my mama. I don't rememba nothin bout that, but bein with Pa on Saturday was bout the onliest thing I looked forward to. That's cause Missy Ann growed into a treacherous child. She was mean in her spirit and I wasn't allowed to do nothin to oppose her, which only made her meaner. I swear that gal was born without no conscience a'tall.

Sometimes, when she was in a temper, she'd slap me. The first time, I was only three and didn't know better, so I slapped her back. Missy Ann, she run out cryin to Mistriss Sarah and Mistriss Sarah switched me good. Didn't ask me what happened, or say nothin. Jus come into the room, grabbed me up by the hair and whacked my legs with a hickory switch. Then she walked out the room like I wasn't no more than a dog she found chewin on the rug.

Course, I didn't hit Missy Ann no more. I wasn't a fool altogether. But Mistriss Sarah had herself a bigger story to tell and I was slow to git the message. Fact, I wasn't allowed to frustrate that child in any way. Fact, I was some kinda way responsible for her happiness, all day and all night, too. I slep on a pallet at the foot of her bed and Lord have mercy if she cried in the night.

How I was sposed to care for Missy Ann every hour of the day or night was a mystery I didn't git. Like I could never figure why Mista Sewell and Masta Harris blamed a hungry slave for pickin a few melons. But I understands much better now. I was trainin to be a slave, like Pa trained them two-year-old horses to the saddle. I would live my whole life at the foot of Missy Ann's bed. I would care for her chirrens. I would serve her till one of us died.

Over time, specially when she was young, Missy Ann and me would play together. She didn't have no choice, since there weren't no other chirrens to play with. But her kinda play was to use me like she was usin her dolls when she held her tea parties at the little table in her room. I'd line up between her dolls like I was a doll myself. Then she'd tell me what to say and how to act. Sometimes I was the bad doll and I had to be punished. Course, I didn't like takin punishment from a girl who couldn't lace up her own shoes. But it was a heap better than gettin switched.

Ceptin for visitin Pa on Saturday nights, the other thing I looked forward to was church on Sunday mornins. Mosly, Masta Harris didn't want his slaves gatherin together, even if they was gatherin to worship the Lord. Masta Harris figured they was gonna make some kinda uprisin. I don't know what he thought they was gonna rise up with, sticks and stones? But him and all the slaveholders was scared to death bout slave rebellions that took place further east. That's why they organized the patrollers.

The patrollers—mos slaves called em patterollers—rode every night, lookin for slaves who was off their plantations without a pass signed by their masta. When the patrollers caught one, they would give em a good whippin and bring em back to the farm they come from. Then, the masta mos likely whipped em again. Still, some slaves, they had wives or chirrens livin on other farms and they would sneak off to be with em, whippin or no.

The house slaves was the ception to this rule. Masta and Mistriss and Missy Ann couldn't no way be without their personal slaves. Masta had ol Isaiah, who tended Masta wherever he went. And Mistriss Sarah, she pretty near couldn't dress herself without Winnie. And Missy Ann? Why she'd pitch a fit if I was left behind. So, when the family went to church, we all went with em. Course, we had to sit up in the gallery and not downstairs with the white folks, but we didn't mind that none. Fact, we mosly didn't wanna be round white folks no way.

Reverend Crutchfield preached long and hard on Sunday mornins, holdin up his Bible, dancin round like ants was bitin him all over his body. Us in the gallery, we didn't git too rambunctious, didn't sing too loud or nothin. Partly that was cause Reverend Crutchfield would preach to the slaves at the end of the service. He'd tell us that Jesus wanted us to always mind our mastas and never steal nothin and never run away. He'd say if we do jus like masta tells us, we gonna go up to some kinda slave heaven.

Natrally, we all wasn't no way prayin to git into slave heaven. No, sir. We was prayin for a Moses to lead us outta slavery. Far as we was concerned, Masta and all his like was little Pharaohs, holdin God's peoples in bondage. Even to this day, I sometimes think the Good Lord has got Himself a mighty fine sense of humor. That's cause our Moses turned out to be a white man name of Abraham Lincoln.

But that there is another story than the one I'm after tellin, so I believes I'll jus save it for another day. Meanwhiles, I got beans need snappin and a chicken I gotta pluck and a fire to make if my family's gonna have dinner this evenin. Ophelia be comin back from work pretty soon, and she is one gal who appreciates havin her dinner on time.

Chapter 4

WHY ME?

MOM WOKE ME up at seven o'clock in the morning. "Maddie," she said from the door of my room, "you awake, honey? Your dad's on the phone. He wants to talk to you."

I was exhausted. My sleep had been full of weird dreams that slid away at the sound of my mother's voice and headed for some deep place where I wasn't allowed to go. I was a little confused, too, drawn to Mom's voice and to my fleeting dreams at the same time. Then I remembered that Dr. Rosenberg had prescribed medicine to prevent another seizure and that I'd taken a dose last night.

"You'll need to monitor the side effects of the Dilantin," he'd told my mother. "Fatigue is the most common symptom. Fatigue and some confusion, especially on wakening. Depending on the individual, these effects can be quite severe, but they generally diminish over time."

Generally? I mean, talk about weasel words. Still, I was glad to be awake. It meant I was alive.

"It's okay, Mom. I'm up." I took the phone and held it to my ear. "Hi, Daddy."

My dad's voice was cheery, but then he was always cheery. My friends called him *Silver Lining*. "Baby, how are you?"

"A little sleepy," I admitted, "but everything's working just fine."

"That's wonderful. I'll be catching a flight late this afternoon. I should be home around noon tomorrow."

My father jumping on the next plane out? Was I seriously on death's door? If so, why wasn't anyone telling me?

"You should wait until after the MRI. It might not be anything. I mean, it's not like I'm sick. I feel great and the doctor said it might not be…"

That was as far as I got. It was like the words *brain* and *tumor* were erased from my vocabulary. But Dad understood well enough to offer a little comfort.

"No, no, honey. The bulk of my work here is finished, and I've been looking for a reason to get away. Let somebody else dot the i's and cross the t's. So, thank you for providing me with a good excuse. I'm sure I won't be needed by the time I get home. In fact, if the weather's not too cold, I may just do some fly fishing."

Dad was a big-time trout fisherman. I used to go with him sometimes. It was kind of fun until I finally caught a fish and saw the hook going through its mouth. Then I had a why-am-I-torturing-this-little-creature moment. I could feel the barb tearing at my own mouth as I watched my father remove the hook and release the fish. After that I was like, excuse me, but I'll take my fish on a plate, thank you very much.

"All right, Daddy, I'll see you when you get home. Love you."

To tell the truth, I was happy that he was coming home. Relieved, really. Between him and Mom, I felt that there wasn't anything they couldn't take care of. Especially me. Especially *now*.

Mom had breakfast sitting on the breakfast bar when I came out of the bathroom. Waffles, my favorite—which I imagine was supposed to make me feel comforted, but gave me the opposite feeling instead. Was I the condemned girl eating a hearty meal before being led to the electric chair?

"So, Maddie, what did you think about your great-great-great-grandmother's story?" Mom asked with a strained air of casualness. *I* knew she wanted to ask how I was feeling. But *she* knew I hated to be fussed over.

I poured maple syrup on my waffle and swished it around with my fork. When one of your parents asks a question like that, you just know there's a specific answer they want to hear. But the truth was that I didn't know what to think of the memoir yet, and I finally asked a question of my own.

"How old were you when you read Golden Lea Jackson's memoir?"

Mom grew silent. She looked at me out of the corner of her eye, the way she does when she thinks I'm up to something. But I just maintained my *who, me?* expression. Besides, I wanted to know why Mom had picked now to pass on this legacy. Like, was this my last chance to read it? Now or never? And you can't blame me for thinking that way. Parents hide the truth from their kids all the time.

"I didn't get to read Golden Lea's *Recollections* until I was older, in my first year at law school," Mom finally

45

said. "And I wasn't doing all that well. College? I just sort of breezed through Rutgers and I guess I thought I was some kind of hotshot. But law school is another story. Especially at New York University, where they were trying to compete with Yale and Harvard. The workload was crushing, baby. There weren't enough hours in the day and I was barely keeping my head above water. I was getting very discouraged. That was when Gramma let me read Golden Lea's *Recollections.*"

Mom opened the waffle maker and plopped a golden brown waffle on her plate. She poured herself a cup of coffee, added milk and a packet of sweetener, then came over to join me. I think she wanted to drop the subject. Barely keeping her head above water was, like, totally against her Alpha self-image. Too bad. Her imperfections made me relate to her more.

"Why then?" I wondered out loud.

"I asked Gramma that very question, but you know Gramma."

"She's not big on explaining herself."

"Exactly. In the end, though, I got the point without an explanation. Golden Lea's story is all about fighting those long, hard odds. Talk about a stacked deck. Growing up black thirty years ago was no bed of roses, but it was a million times better than being a slave. Golden Lea Jackson, though, she never gave up."

Mom sipped at her coffee. "But that's enough of that. What Golden Lea's story did for me is irrelevant. You've got to find its meaning for yourself. And we, meaning you and I, have to get out of here. We've got an eight-thirty appointment in Manhattan."

"In Manhattan?" The sad truth was that I didn't have clue one. I remembered Mom being on the phone for hours, but the final result was a total blank.

"Baby," Mom said, "do you know what's going to happen today?"

"Take an MRI?" I guessed.

"Do you know where?"

Talk about embarrassing. I mean, *puh-leeeze*. We were talking about my brain here. The least I could have done was pay attention.

"Not a clue, Mom."

Mom tossed me one of those patented I-thought-so looks. "We're going to the Samuelson Hospital for Pediatric Neurology in Manhattan. It's rated the best neurology center on the East Coast. And the doctor we're consulting, Anthony Balder, has been listed in *Best Doctors* for the past fifteen years."

The little speech was supposed to be reassuring, but the word I focused on was "hospital." I mean, why not a doctor's office? Forget "pediatric." I had already come to terms with that. And neurology? Don't even get me started on how many ways that creeps me out. But the worst thing about it all was that I hated the *smell* of hospitals. They smelled like sickness.

But the doorbell rang before I could even raise the "hospital" issue. It was Maria, our housekeeper. She was a young woman, not more than twenty-five years old, and she worked harder than anybody I knew. She had a routine, too, that she stuck with no matter what, a routine that started in the kitchen.

Naturally, we couldn't talk with Maria there and maybe that was for the best. I mean, there wasn't really anything to talk about, right? At least, nothing I wanted to talk about… Not before I took the MRI.

Driving into Manhattan during rush hour was like fighting a war in slow motion. We were heading for northern Manhattan. Fifth Avenue and 108th Street, to be exact. Our route took us along the I-80 freeway to the Jersey turnpike, then over the George Washington Bridge into Manhattan and then down to 125th Street. Us and about ten million commuters. And the funny part was that when we finally got off at 125th Street—between the buses, the trucks, and the double-parked cars—the traffic was even worse. It took us twenty minutes to go four blocks.

But the traffic gave me plenty of time to think—about everything *except* where we were headed. We were driving on Harlem's main drag and the sidewalks were crowded mostly with black and brown human beings. I've already described how I fit into the scheme of things in affluent Montclair, and how I reacted to being called an Oreo. But that doesn't mean I wasn't trying to figure out who I was.

I knew that most people would take one look at me and decide that I probably was black. But that didn't seem right to me. Like, if a black poodle and a white Labrador had puppies together, nobody would say the puppies were black poodles. So if a black human being and a white human being have a baby together, why is the baby automatically black? I mean, gimme a break.

But Harlem wasn't Montclair, not by a long shot. I could stroll through Harlem and never feel out of place.

The faces of the people walking along the sidewalk and crossing the street were of every color when you looked close. But I doubted that many of them would question their identity.

So, who was I? My mom was a very opinionated woman, one of those people who think they know everything about everything. But she'd never forced any labels on me, much to her credit. Still, that left me in limbo. That left me dancing on a tightrope. Fall one way and you're black, fall the other way and you're white.

There was one comforting fact, though, which I discovered while doing research for a report. In the 2000 U.S. Census, seven million people identified themselves as multiracial. I wanted to compare that number to the number who checked off the box in 1990. But there was no multiracial category in 1990, or in any other census before 2000. Before 2000, the way the government counted you, you were either white, black, Latino, Asian, American Indian, or Polynesian. Now it was possible to be more what you really were. I just hoped I'd have the chance to figure it all out...

The thing about pediatrics is that it includes everyone from infants to seventeen-year-olds. So if you're a pediatrician and you're decorating your office, who do you decorate for? Infants, toddlers, pre-adolescents, teenagers? Samuelson Hospital had pitched its decor to the younger set. Lots of white clouds and green meadows, lambs and puppy dogs, Sesame Street Muppets and Barney cutouts.

Although part of me seemed to be sleepwalking through this nightmare, another part was hyperaware of my surroundings. If anyone had asked me what I was wearing at that moment, I wouldn't have been able to answer (Jasmine would be *so* ashamed). I could only have *hoped* that I remembered to put on pants that morning, much less bothered to match. But the faint smell of antiseptic and germs wafting through the air that no one else seemed to notice? My nostrils registered that in the first five seconds. And the Bert and Ernie pictures on the walls of my examining room? Those may be burned into my memory for the rest of my life. And if that's the case, why couldn't it at least have been two cute guys, like Edward and Jacob from the *Twilight* movie?

Needless to say, I was, like, depressed before the door closed behind me. I mean, I couldn't count the number of times I'd been lectured on taking responsibility. You're not a child anymore. That was the message. So why did I have to come to a child's hospital? Why did I have to be treated like a little kid?

One good thing: I didn't have all that much time to think about it. We were thirty minutes late because of the traffic on 125th Street and the MRI machine was booked solid for the rest of the day. Plus, I had to do a bunch of tests beforehand. That meant more blood taken and another trip to the bathroom with a little cup, of course, but also an EKG to check my heart and an EEG to measure my brain waves. And, oh, yes, did I mention blood pressure and temperature and pulse all in addition to the MRI? Where was the machine to track how many other machines I'd already been hooked up to? I mean, gimme a break, enough already!

Even before this relay race of medical procedures, I was already tired because of the pills I was taking. The tests just stripped off any spare energy I might have had, which means I went through the exams with all the responsiveness of a zombie. And trust me, that was probably a *good* thing.

But the nurses and technicians? They were nonstop. Nice, but in a hurry, just like in the emergency room the day before. I half expected to see them hooked up to their own individual IV machines that dripped Red Bull straight into their bloodstreams.

When the exams were over—they were a complete blur to me—I was ushered back into the waiting area, which was just as crowded as the one in the ER. Only now, I was face to face with kids who were in treatment. Kids with scraggly patches of hair. Skinny, pale kids who looked like they were at death's door. Kids who trembled. Kids with surgical scars that crisscrossed their scalps. I even saw a kid with one eye. She couldn't have been more than seven years old.

I guess I should have been afraid, but for some strange reason, I wasn't. I was more sympathetic than scared. Besides, I had convinced myself that there was nothing wrong with me, nothing beyond that magical inflammation Dr. Rosenberg spoke about. Or maybe multiple sclerosis. I didn't know exactly what multiple sclerosis was, just like I didn't know what an inflammation was, but I was sure they were both better than a brain tumor, even without having Googled them. And I clung desperately to that diagnosis, preparing myself to hear it from the doctor, picturing the way his mouth would pronounce the words. *Inflammation. Multiple sclerosis.* I would probably hug my mother, then jump for joy, then do a little victory dance like a football player who just scored a winning touchdown at the Super Bowl.

I had been too tired all morning to argue, so I let myself be shuffled through all of those unnecessary tests and hooked up to all of those machines, but they'd see soon. I always did well on tests, and these would be no exception. I'd ace them, too, and come out with a clean bill of health.

I wouldn't even allow myself to *think* that a brain tumor was possible. It was something that happened to other people, like these poor kids in the waiting room. I'm not saying that it was fair that they had it. It wasn't *fair* at all—the furthest thing from it. Just that anyone who looked at them could see they were sick. But other than a few freak incidents, and some side effects and drowsiness from the drugs, I felt fine. Like my old self. Not sick. Not like them.

My mom, though? She was having trouble looking at those other kids. Every one of them had mothers who had probably reacted just as stubbornly as mine had. "Brain tumor? Not my child. I'll fix it somehow. I won't let anything happen." But it *did* happen—to their children. And there was nothing they could do about it. Not all the love in the world, not all the phone calls they made or the appointments with the best doctors could change the fact that their kids had gotten sick, unfair as it was. And I could see that that randomness, that unfairness, terrified my mother, though she tried her hardest *not* to let me see it.

So every once in awhile, I reached out to pat Mom's hand. She was having a really hard time. I could tell from the way she held her mouth, with her lips compressed, and the way she stared down at the same page of her book for half an hour at a time, without so much as a glance up so she wouldn't have to see those sick kids. I'm sure that as a mother, just the thought of them broke her heart, never mind the possibility of her child being among them. The least I could do was to try to make her feel better, especially since I kept thinking that it was all my fault she had to be there in the first place.

It was almost noon before I finished all the preliminary testing, and a nurse had me change into a hospital gown and remove my earrings and any other metal I might have been hiding. It was time for the big exam.

The paper-thin gown exposed more than enough, but as I handed over the small gold hoops that my parents had given me for my thirteenth birthday, I felt totally stripped bare and vulnerable. All my certainty that I'd be fine melted away in that instant. In fact, I didn't even feel like Maddie anymore. I felt like just another body ready for examination: no clothes, no earrings, no personal belongings, no identifying marks—no individuality. And you know that my motto as a Mag-7 was "Individuality or death." Some choice.

Suddenly, I remembered my reflection in the mirror: the girl who looked like me but wasn't me. *That's* who I felt like. Trapped behind glass, staring back but utterly mute and unable to run away.

Even though I was wearing only tissue paper, I wanted to run out to my mother in the waiting room—have her hold me again, have her whisper comforting, reassuring words and call me her baby. Instead, some stranger escorted me to the MRI room where yet another nurse put earplugs in my ears and settled a pair of headphones over the plugs.

The scanner itself was gigantic compared to the CT scanner; it was absolutely terrifying just to look at. And this machine didn't just circle my head. It was like a narrow tunnel that circled my whole body. And it made this weird clicking noise that reminded me of insects for some reason—not at the top of my list of favorite things—and a clanging noise that reminded me of cracked church bells. And, of course, I was supposed to stay still. Don't move, don't move. And did I mention that the scan took *forty-five* minutes? And that halfway through I felt like I was suffocating?

Don't move, don't move. Yeah, right. But I did somehow manage to remain still. Maybe because I was scared stiff. Or maybe because I was sure of one thing: If I moved, I'd have to do the scan all over again.

When it was finished, there was nothing left to do but sit in the reception area and wait for the results. I'm pretty sure I didn't move a muscle then, either.

Dr. Anthony Balder was a short, middle-aged black man with a noticeable paunch. His skin was the color of a mocha latte, and he had a spray of darker freckles under each eye and across the bridge of his nose. Like everyone else in the hospital, he looked tired. But he wasn't in a hurry, and his brown eyes, behind his reading glasses, were kind.

We were in his small office, sitting on chairs in front of his desk. In the few fractions of a second it took him to glance at my medical folder and study the shiny MRI printout, my eyes were darting all over the room, trying to soak in every last detail and read the doctor the same way he was reading me. Well-worn medical books. Diploma from one of my Ivy League dream schools. Framed pictures of his pretty wife and adorable, smiling kids. A full life. The kind I wanted.

Then I stole a look at the MRI printout on his desk. I was still trying to see the bright side. To me, the white spot on this scan looked almost exactly like the white spot on the CT scan. At least it hadn't gotten any bigger.

"I'm afraid the news isn't good." Dr. Balder's deep voice rumbled up from his chest, shattering my fragile hopes. "I wish I could tell you otherwise, but I can't."

Bam! My stomach sunk to my knees, like right before I go down a huge drop on a roller coaster. Just like I learned to do on Space Mountain at Disneyland, I squeezed my eyes shut and balled my fists up tight, picturing myself somewhere safe and stable—at home on my comfortable sofa with the TV turned all the way up—instead of spiraling downward, out of control, fighting the urge to throw up.

Only this wasn't an amusement ride—this was *my life*. And the only way I could deal with the doctor's isn't-good news was by jumping right back into denial. Every word he said after "*afraid*" simply vanished. Now you hear it, now you don't.

But Dr. Balder had been delivering bad news for a long time and he knew all about denial. He spoke to me directly, with no blame in his voice—only a firmness that forced me off my imaginary sofa and back again into his office, where I had no TV to drown him out and no choice but to deal with the facts.

"Maddie, did you hear what I just said?" he asked.

I opened my eyes, glanced at my mother, then looked straight at the doctor for a full three seconds before looking down. "I... I... No."

"You have a tumor, Maddie, about the size of a raisin, in the left temporal lobe of your brain." He slid a plastic model of the human brain to the center of his desk, then removed a big chunk about the size and shape of a small loaf of bread. I wanted to look away again, but couldn't. Whether or not it was good news, someone was *finally* trying to explain what was going on inside me.

"This is the left temporal lobe. It's responsible for speech, memory, and hearing, and to a lesser extent, balance and coordination. Your tumor is in this section, where the temporal lobe meets the frontal lobe," the doctor said, pointing to the model.

Looking at it close up like that made me feel squeamish, like seeing a dissected frog in science class. But that healthy plastic brain, as gross as it was, wasn't anything compared to my own squishy, sick brain with the awful white spot that the MRI showed so clearly. In fact, as the doctor spoke, I could swear I felt the tumor growing inside those lobes that I just learned about.

Mom picked that moment to jump in—and I was surprised she'd waited that long. Sometimes her constant questions were annoying. This time, though, it was as if her voice brought me back from someplace far away to remind me I really wasn't in this alone.

"What kind of tumor is it?" she asked.

Dr. Balder stifled a grin. My mom had been doing research on the computer the night before, trying to stay a step ahead. She was just like my friends or me, Googling like crazy to become instant experts for our school presentations. Over the course of a few hours, she basically convinced herself that she had gone to medical school, gotten her degree and knew as much as any doctor. This was another syndrome, like denial, that Dr. Balder had dealt with before. Instead of addressing my mom, he turned to me when he answered.

"Questions like benign or malignant can't be answered with an MRI. Nor can an MRI tell whether a tumor is primary or secondary. Primary means the tumor arose in the brain. Secondary means it spread from somewhere else. Do you understand, Maddie?"

When Dr. Balder paused, I proved that I didn't by changing the subject. All I really understood, from Spanish class, was that "mal" meant "bad"—and that was enough information for me. Okay, I'm chicken. So, sue me.

"What causes a…a brain tumor?" I asked.

"The simple answer is that science has yet to answer that question. No link to smoking or diet or lifestyle has ever been made."

"So, *I* could have done something wrong. *I* could be to blame, only you don't know how?"

Dr. Balder wasn't fooled. I was trying to act like there were *reasons* behind it—like if I could only figure out what I'd done wrong and fix it, I'd have this thing under control in no time. Essentially, I was acting like my mother.

But the truth was that I couldn't control it, which was the scary part. From this point on, my brain was in the hands of the doctors and nurses who'd work on me. But I wasn't ready to accept that yet. In fact, I wanted to think about anything *except* what came next. I mean, my eyes were bouncing around the room again like they were on springs, searching for distractions. Where were Bert and Ernie when you really needed them?

Trying to pull me back into the present moment again, Dr. Balder leaned forward and looked directly into my eyes, addressing me like an adult. "You've got a hard road ahead of you, Maddie. If it's any consolation, many others have been down this road, too."

"And lived to tell about it?"

"Maddie!" My mom was like, omigosh, how could a daughter of mine say such a thing? Maybe she was worried about the jinx, too.

But Dr. Balder only laughed, a hearty rumble every bit as deep as his speaking voice. "Yes, Maddie, and lived to tell about it. At least the ones who went to other doctors."

It took me a second, but then I was laughing, too. Mom joined in a moment later. A sense of humor wasn't such a bad thing for a doctor to have. In fact, even more than his Ivy League medical degree, it gave me hope.

But if I was ready to face up to the future, that didn't mean I was happy about it. I mean, what did I do to deserve a brain tumor? At home, I was a responsible role model. I kept up my grades and I was the best girl basketball player in the school. So why me? I knew a couple of girls— self-proclaimed Alphas—who had already tried smoking cigarettes. And one of my best friends, Marsha the Nerd, practically lived on Gummy Bears and Hershey Kisses. It was a miracle she was even growing.

Then something else occurred to me, something really, really obvious. What did Golden Lea Jackson do to deserve being a slave? Except be born?

"Maddie?"

I looked up as Dr. Balder took off his reading glasses. "Yes, sir?"

"We need to discuss treatment." He waited for me to nod, then went on to explain my two options. Dr. Balder could attempt to remove the tumor through surgery. That sounded great. Here today and hot tamale.

Unfortunately, he explained, there was the distinct possibility that my tumor couldn't be completely removed. It was lying in a very delicate spot, so delicate that removing it might cause more damage than leaving it where it was. The second option, which he recommended, was to obtain a tissue sample through a needle biopsy. Many tumors, especially in the young, he told me, are very slow growing. Once the tumor was identified, the best approach might be to watch and wait.

Do I have to say which option we finally chose? Do you take dumb pills in the morning? Watch and wait? Talk about throw-your-poor-doggie-a-bone. Plus, it was Thursday and the biopsy wouldn't be performed until Saturday, which at least gave me one day off. True, the procedure was nasty to the max. Dr. Balder would drill a hole the size of a dime in my skull, then jam a needle into my brain. Just the thought of it sent shivers down my spine. But it was nothing compared to a full-scale craniotomy.

Okay, so maybe I was back to denial. But you can't blame me. I didn't invent watch-and-wait, after all. From Dr. Balder's office, we went to the hospital pharmacy, where I picked up two prescriptions: an antibiotic to prevent post-op infection and a steroid to prevent post-op swelling. Then we went home to a dinner of grilled chicken breasts, wild rice and salad. I didn't taste a bite of it, although I somehow managed to empty my plate.

My dad called around seven. He was in Lisbon, waiting on a connection that would bring him into Philadelphia at nine o'clock in the morning. We had a long conversation in which I used the phrase "watch and wait" at least twenty times. Then he was gone and I was suddenly very, very tired. That was a side effect of the medicine. Yet at the same time, my brain was zipping right along. That was a side effect of my nerves.

Call me yo-yo girl.

I went to my room after hanging up with my dad and text-messaged my friends. I might have called them, but I really didn't want to go through the whole "watch and wait" thing again, especially since it would only make them worry. Besides, I had something else on my mind. I wanted to read the next part of Golden Lea Jackson's story. Dr. Balder said I'd be walking down a hard road for some time to come. Would it be harder than Golden Lea's?

Somehow, I doubted it.

Chapter 5

PRAYER AND
A PLAN

*M*ISSY ANN DIDN'T *git no sweeter as she growed. No, sir, not on no account. Fact, once she come to understand that I'd git my legs switched if she so much as blinked her pretty blue eyes, she started in to makin threats against me. If I didn't do this or didn't do that, she'd tell on me. I thought this was a might dumb on accounta I was already a slave and one lesson a slave learns early in life is never say no. And I do mean never.*

You might trick masta and git by with it. You might sometimes say, Yes, Masta, and not do what you were tole. Then, you was jus a rascal. But there wasn't no masta on the face of this good Earth would tolerate impudence from a slave. Now I have heard tell of some mastas that didn't hold with whippin their slaves. The peoples who tole me this said their mastas was right kind. But they also said if a slave was no account or impudent, their mastas would right away sell em to a masta who wasn't scared of the whip. Fact, some mastas I heard bout had themselfs a reputation for breakin impudent slaves.

But I wasn't in no danger of gettin sold, at least back then. Me and Missy Ann, we was little and Missy Ann was still attached to me. That was how come I started goin to church. Also, after a time, Mistriss Sarah come to figure out how things was with her daughter. Mistriss Sarah, she wasn't what you might call a natral parent anyway. Her and Masta was mosly busy with entertainin. There was always peoples stayin at Belle Maison. And many a time, when the bedrooms was full, we'd have twenty peoples to dinner.

Them dinners, they was somethin. The kitchen slaves would start early in the mornin. They'd polish the chandeliers and fix em with new candles. Then they'd polish the silverware and wipe down the good china dishes and hot iron the linens and clean the crystal till it shined. And the peoples would dress up in their finest, the womens all in gowns and wearin their bes jewelry. The entrance was like a parade, mens and womens arm in arm, the mens pullin out chairs. I rememba one of them dinners had sixteen courses. There was three kinds of soup, and there was pork and chicken and beef and venison and fish straight from the creek. And enough brandy to fill that there creek.

Missy Ann didn't take no part in them dinners, not till she got a lot older. She wasn't wanted and we'd mosly sit on the back porch while they was goin on. Cook would come out while we was there—I rememba this like I remembas my own name—carryin buckets of mush. She'd walk down the steps and across the yard to the troughs where the slave chirrens ate. All the time shoutin, "Come and git it, come and git it."

And them kids would come from everywhere, runnin cross the yard like a pack of dogs.

The way I come to read and write was thisaway. There weren't no school near Belle Maison, least not one Masta Harris wanted to send his only child to. So what he done was hire himself a tutor. Her name was Miss Andrea Colbert and she was a woman who could use her tongue like Mista Sewell used the whip. The first time she said, "Missy Ann, you are dumb as a stick," Missy Ann ran direct to her mama.

"Mama, mama, Miss Colbert say I'm dumb as a stick."

That was the onliest time I ever saw Mistriss Sarah take a hand to her child. But she smacked Missy Ann's behind till that girl was cryin like a baby. Then she sent Missy Ann right back to Miss Colbert. And me, I knowed this ain't too Christian, but it was all I could do not to bust out laughin.

Missy Ann never did run to her mama after that day. But she didn't learn much, neither. I knowed bout this cause I was in the room while she was havin her lessons. Jus in case she needed somethin. Masta, he didn't truck with slaves learnin to read and write. I rememba one night he come sneakin round the cabins and caught a slave named of Jemmi readin a book. Come the mornin, Masta dragged Jemmi all the way to the slave pens in Louisville and sold him off.

Masta Harris weren't no different than any other masta when it come to slaves learnin anythin ceptin how to count. They was afraid the slaves would pass messages between the plantations and there would be an uprisin. I never did see the sense of it, cause if the slaves was gonna plan an uprisin, they wouldn't be dumb enough to write their plans on no paper.

But Masta was Masta, and he didn't have to make no sense. He jus had to say what he wanted and that was it. Slaves was not to learn their letters, not the field hands, nor the stable grooms, nor the house slaves. Learnin was for white peoples only.

So while Missy Ann was gettin her lessons from Miss Colbert, I was put to mendin shifts, which was what slave chirrens wore till they was old enough to go out in the fields. A shift weren't no more than a big shirt made of homespun cotton that come down to the knees. As a house slave, I wore a reglar dress and had good shoes, but all the rest of the chirrens wore shifts and went barefoot mos all the way through the winter.

Patchin shifts ain't no big thing. Them chirrens wasn't bout to complain if my stitches wasn't straight, or even if the patch fell right off. And I was pretty good with a needle for a girl that age. I could stitch right along and still listen to Missy Ann's lessons. That's how I come to learn my letters faster than Missy Ann. I was a year older than her, of course, and natrally able to take more in.

Now Missy Ann, on top of not bein as smart as she might be, was a lazy child. Till she was mos five years old, I was the one dressed her. Not cause she couldn't dress herself, but cause she didn't want to. But she weren't no fool and hardly a month went by till she figures out I can read. Then she has me teach her in private. So, on top of listenin in, I was readin from Missy Ann's books and doin my numbers right alongside her.

After that, Missy Ann became Miss Colbert's little scholar.

Things went along thisaway for near bout two years. Then one day, Missy Ann, for no reason whatsoever, went and tole on me. The way it happened was thisaway. Masta Harris and Mistriss Sarah was right sticklers for doin the proper thing. And one thing that was proper was that they should spend some time with their child. Iffen they likes her or not. So mos every afternoon, round five o'clock, I would git Missy Ann dressed and take her to visit her folks in the parlor.

Them was long hours. Missy and me would play some kinda game, while Masta and Mistriss had a glass of that port wine they drank fore dinner. Masta and Mistriss mosly talked bout the plantation and who was comin to dinner and Masta Harris's travelin schedule. Masta Harris was spendin heaps of time in Frankfort, which is the capitol of Kentucky. That's when he wasn't off to Louisville or Lexington on business. Mistriss Sarah wanted him to stay home more. She didn't trust the overseer, Mista Sewell. Claimed he was stealin a piece of the tobacco crop and sellin it off to a small farmer who lived over east of Belle Maison. Masta, he would jus sit there, noddin his head and smokin his pipe. Say, "Yes, dear, yes, dear."

Now this particular afternoon weren't no different than any other afternoon. Not far as I can see. So there weren't no reason for Missy Ann to do what she done ceptin for pure meanness. Missy Ann had jus turned nine years old, so I guess I was near bout ten.

We was sittin at a table, playin draughts. Since I come north, I hear the game is called checkers, but at Belle Maison it was called draughts. Course, I was losin, like always. I wasn't no fool, neither. Then Missy, outta nowhere, up and said, "Mommy, do you know that Golden Lea can read?"

Lands, the commotion. First, Masta Harris asked Missy Ann if she was lyin. That brought Missy Ann to start bawlin. How could her own mama and papa ever say such a thing bout their little girl? Then Mistriss Sarah turned to me.

"Golden Lea, can you read?"

What was I gonna say now? Say Missy Ann ain't tellin the truth? I was gonna be Missy Ann's slave for life. Iffen I lied on her, there wouldn't be no end to the matter. But iffen I owned up to knowin my letters, I knew I'd git switched real hard. This wasn't like the problems in Missy's arithmetic book. This was a problem didn't have no solution. Finally, I jus gave up.

65

"*Yes'um, jus a might,*" *I said.*

Masta Harris looked at me hard, then tole Missy Ann to fetch one of her little story books. Missy Ann, she stopped bawlin and skipped out the room like ain't nothin happened. When she come back, she was carryin her favorite book, The Sheep in the Meadow.

"*Here, Golden Lea,*" *she said,* "*show Mama and Papa how you can read.*"

Well, I was in for it then. Yes, sir, I was shoved right into a corner and there wasn't no way out. So what I done, was read jus as proud as I could. I read every word and I read em a sight faster than Missy Ann ever did.

When I stopped, Masta Harris spoke up to his daughter. "*Ann, how did Golden Lea learn to read?*"

"*I don't know, Daddy.*"

Masta Harris turned to me then. "*Golden Lea, how did you learn to read?*"

I knowed what was gonna happen next and I don't mind sayin I busted out cryin. If I tole the truth and said that Missy Ann taught me so I could help her with her lessons, Missy Ann woulda mos likely got punished. But I knew I wouldn't escape, neither. I knew I'd git switched jus to teach me to act better in the future.

So what I done was say, "*I learnt watchin Missy Ann when she was takin her lessons from Miss Colbert.*"

I got switched natrally, switched harder than I ever been switched in my life. And Missy Ann, she gotta watch, this bein a good lesson for her on how to treat slaves. I swear there's nights when I can still see her grinnin, jus as happy as a lark. But she wasn't grinnin a month later when she went back to bein dumb as a stick.

That there switchin didn't stop me from readin, neither. See, Missy Ann, she was right scared of the dark. Had to have a candle burnin all night long. And woe to me if I let that candle burn down without lightin up another one. After I stopped hurtin and started thinkin more clear, I seen this candle was my bes chance. Missy Ann slep deep. She never woke up at night. And Masta and Mistriss, there weren't no reason for them to check up on their child cause I was there to do it for em. So late at night, while Missy Ann snored in her bed, I'd study in her books. Lands, I rememba them times so well. Listenin to the bullfrogs on a summer night, and the hootin of an owl and the bark of a fox. I would read till my eyes was near mos fallin outta my head. Tryin to learn everything there was fore the sun come up. The only things I regrets is that I didn't have hardly a chance to practice my letters. I was scared to write anything down lessen Missy Ann would find the papers.

I can't say what Masta woulda done if he caught me readin again. I spect he woulda put me outta Belle Maison in a right hurry. But I had me a purpose for takin such a risk and it weren't no trivial purpose, neither. Since I started goin to church with Missy Ann, I was bein more and more drawn to the Spirit of the Lord. Jus like a sewin needle to them little magnets Missy Ann played with. And I wasn't the only one, neither. My pa, Elijah, and Masta Harris's coachman, Tom, was also drawn to the Lord. And there was plenty among the field hands, who was hungry for the teachin.

Now Tom couldn't read nor write, but he had himself a Bible. Said he got it from a slave in Louisville. Me, I was mos anxious to study up on that Bible and learnin my letters was how I done it. Then on Saturday nights, I'd read Bible stories to Pa and Tom and some of the other hands. At first, I went real slow. There was many a word in that Good Book I ain't never heard before. But after a time, we learned to puzzle out the meanins and we gotta havin a reglar prayer service, all the time watchin to see that Masta wasn't sneakin round. And what we prayed for mos of the time, was deliverance.

Course, takin risks for the Lord ain't nothin new. The prophets and the apostles, they was always riskin their lives, and more than one died for his faith. Now I ain't sayin we was riskin our own lives. Mos the time, slaves was too valuable to outright kill. But Masta woulda whipped us good, at the very least, if he caught us. We knowed all that very well, but we was determined to learn the ways of the Lord who delivered the Israelites from bondage. And little by little, the Lord came to be a great comfort to me. In time of trouble, I turned to Him and he never did disappoint. No, sir. When my heart was hurtin, He was always there.

I was only a young girl, bout twelve years old, when Preacher Haskill brought his revival to Clark County. This was the biggest thing happened in many a year. Preacher Haskill was a famous man and there was those said he could outtalk Satan himself.

Now some mastas was allowin their slaves to go to the three-day revival and some wasn't. Masta Harris he was on the side that said religion ain't meant for slaves, but he made a ception for the house slaves he let go to church. He never did give no reason. Jus cided how it was gonna be and that was that.

I felt bad for my pa and I was thinkin on stayin home. But my daddy tole me to go on ahead and I'm happy to this day that I did. The preacher, he preached for two days, preached to more peoples than I ever seen in my life. All singin and shoutin till they was too hoarse to do more than squawk. Natrally, the white folk was in front, while the slaves had to stand in back up on the hill. But I didn't pay that no mind. The Lord's Spirit was runnin through me like a wind and I couldn't no more stop it than I could stop the beatin of my own heart.

On the third day, the preacher called for all the sinners to come down to the river and be baptized. And I was sho ready when he did. I waded out into the water till it come up to my waist and let the preacher take hold of me.

"Girl, are you ready to receive the Lord Jesus in your heart?"

"Yes, sir, I am surely ready."

Preacher Haskill pinched my nose and bent me back till my head was under the water. That very minute I felt the Spirit dive down into my soul. I felt the Spirit take possession and I heard the Lord speak directly to my heart.

"You are mine now, girl, and I will never let you loose."

Well, saved or not, the years kep on goin by and there was many a time I half-wished that it was Masta Harris gone under the water stead of me. Or Mistriss Sarah or Missy Ann. Them folks sure needed savin, but they didn't see it that way. No, sir. They thought they was good Christians, but the truth was they didn't care bout nothin but themselfs and money.

The reason how I come to know this was that the family was never without their personal slaves. Masta Harris had Isaiah, had em since Isaiah was a boy. Mistriss Sarah, she had Winnie, and Missy Ann had me. Since we was there mos all the time, we natrally heard the family talk and what they mosly talked bout was money. How much they was spendin and how much the crop would fetch and the price of slaves and land. These was folks who lived to put on a show. Good example be the horses we bred. Them horses never made no money for Masta

Harris, not a single dollar. And they was grazin on land that mighta been used to plant a crop that did make money.

But Masta Harris, he jus gotta have his thorobreds. Jus gotta. And them horses is what finally led me and my pa to run away. This happened when I was near to be fourteen years old. The price of tobacco had dropped down to where the leaf wasn't even worth takin to market. But the bills never stopped comin. Belle Maison was heavy mortgaged and Mistriss Sarah didn't stop buyin. New plates, new crystal, new rugs for the parlor and dining room, new clothes. I tells you, some nights Masta Harris was near mos given to apoplexy, he got so mad.

"Woman, this has gotta stop."

Things come to a head on the followin summer. There jus weren't enough cash to go round and Masta had himself a choice. He could sell off some of his horses or he could sell off some of his slaves. I guess I don't gotta say which one he picked.

Now slaves, they got all different kinds of value. A common field hand, who couldn't do much more than hoe and plow, would fetch no more than a few hundred dollars at one of them auctions. But slaves what had skills, like blacksmiths and carpenters and trained house slaves, might fetch a thousand dollars or more.

At my age, I sorta knowed this, but it wasn't somethin I dwelt on. Then one night, Masta and Mistriss had Mista Bradford Jenks to dinner. Masta Harris liked to brag that he owned the biggest plantation in Kentucky. I don't know if that was true, but if it was, Mista Jenks, he owned the next biggest.

By then, Missy Ann was allowed to sit at the table when there was guests at Belle Maison, which is how I happened to hear what I heard. Masta Harris was goin on bout the Yankees and how they was ruinin the tobacco business. Mista Jenks was mosly agreein, but wasn't sayin much. Then, over dessert and brandy, Mista Jenks finally spoke up.

"Harris," he say, "that groom you got? Elijah? He sure does know his way around horses. Iffen you ever want to sell him, I'd give fifteen-hundred dollars."

Masta Harris didn't look at me and he didn't say nothin. But I knowed he wouldn't give two thoughts to breakin up me and Pa. That's cause he done sold my mama and broke up other families many a time. Fact, if Masta Harris was even aware that slaves had feelins, he never showed it. Sellin slaves didn't mean no more to him than sellin cattle and a lot less than sellin a horse.

Well, I guess I don't gotta say how Mista Jenks' words near broke my heart. Thinkin bout how I'd be a slave for all of my life was hard enough for a young girl. But losin my pa was somethin I jus could not accept. I knowed I prayed mos through that night and the next, till Saturday come and I tole my daddy what Mista Jenks said.

Now, my pa, he was a Bible-lovin man and the part he loved bes was bout the Israelites escapin from Egypt. We had spoke bout escapin fore, but we knowed if we got caught, we be in for a bad whippin and one or the other would be sold off. Neither one of us didn't want that, so what we done mosly was jus talk. But things was different now.

"Golden Lea, we gotta go soon. We can't wait on Masta Harris, cause he ain't gonna give us no warnin. One day we here and the next we be sold off. We gotta be doin while we can. Now, you been studyin them geography books like I ask you?"

Pa had been on me bout learnin geography since someone tole him that Ohio, which was a free state, was jus north of Kentucky. What Pa wanted to know was how far that was in miles.

"Bes I can reckon, it's bout seventy miles," I tole him.

My pa was a big man, more than six feet, but he was quiet talkin. He didn't have to say how the patrollers was all around or how Masta would summon Mista Alvin Kraft and his bloodhounds.

Alvin Kraft didn't keep no slaves. Didn't need em. He made a livin catchin slaves who run away. Him and his dogs. Them dogs, they was trained real good. I knowed cause I seen them bein trained. Yes, sir. One day Mista Kraft brung his dogs to Belle Maison as a kinda lesson to any slaves who was thinkin bout runnin away.

The way it happened was thisaway. Masta picked a slave name of Marcus. He tells Marcus, "Boy, I'm gonna give you a head start. You run any which way you choose. Cross water, walk fence rails, anything you can think of to cover your smell. But I advise you to keep one thing in mind. When you hear them dogs gettin close, you find a tree and climb up to a high branch. Cause if them dogs catch you on the ground, they will tear you to pieces fore anyone can pull em off."

I guess I don't gotta say what happened next. Masta waited near an hour fore them dogs was givin a piece of Marcus' clothes to smell and set loose. They didn't take no more than a minute to pick up the trail. Howlin and bayin like the devil himself as they lit off cross the fields. And Marcus, he wasn't no fool, neither. When them dogs come on him, he was so far up a big ol beech tree that he coulda near mos touched the clouds.

So them dogs, they was a big problem. Myself, I couldn't see nary a way to git round em. But my daddy, he mighta been quiet talkin, but he was nobody's fool. He jus draw me in close and put his arm round my shoulder.

"Girl," he says, "I got me a plan."

Chapter 6

FIRST YOU CRY

I WOKE UP the next morning feeling great. Except for the burping part. The burping was a side effect of the antibiotic. Just one of those things, right? The antibiotic was supposed to kill any bacteria growing in my brain after the biopsy. Unfortunately, it killed the bacteria in my stomach, too—the ones that helped me digest. It was Mom who reminded me of this when she came into the room with my morning meds—the Dilantin, the steroid, and the belch-producing antibiotic.

"Maddie, I could hear you from downstairs! That's the antibiotic talking."

"Always a lady," I said.

Mom laughed. "Always a lady" was a line Gramma used on her when she was little, a motto for how she was supposed to live her life. Mom didn't care for that idea at all. Her motto was "Always a *woman*." Ladies, in her opinion, had no place in a courtroom.

I swallowed my pills, amazed at how my illness had already made itself at home in my daily routine. "Mom, am I supposed to go to school today?"

Like any other kid, I occasionally tried to get out of school, usually pretending I was sick. But this time I was being sincere. I mean, everything had changed, right? And I was, like, *What am I now? Am I a patient or a middle school student? Am I a teenager or a machine that needs fixing?* Part of me wanted to go to school to see my friends and get back to my normal life. The other part knew that was impossible.

"Actually, I was thinking we'd all go to a movie when your father gets home. And maybe out to dinner afterwards, at Cipio's."

Sounds great, right? Cipio's was my favorite Italian restaurant. And I was sure I'd get to pick the movie, too. But Mom staying home? Daddy flying in all the way from Greece? Dinner at Cipio's? Cipio's was the Bergamos' special-occasions restaurant. So, what was the occasion? Maddie's last meal?

I know I shouldn't have been thinking that way. You're supposed to trust your parents, and Mom and I had already made a pact: She promised to tell me everything, and I promised not to worry too much. Plus, I wasn't an "issues" kind of kid. With me it was more like, *My parents don't have a clue, but their intentions are good.*

Still, I couldn't get these really suspicious thoughts out of my head. They'd made themselves comfortable, like Goldilocks in the house where the three bears lived, and they weren't going anywhere.

I looked at my mom. She was studying me in that hostile-witness way she had, waiting for whatever wise-guy remark would come out of my mouth. "Yo, Mom?"

She blinked twice and her expression softened. "Yes?"

"A movie sounds great. We'll pick one out when I come down for breakfast. Meanwhile…."

I belched again, and headed for the bathroom. The taste in my mouth was truly gross, another one of those side effects. I think I brushed my teeth for twenty minutes before I took a shower and dressed. Then I headed for the computer to e-mail the Mag-7s to let them know how I was doing—and to rub it in that I had weaseled my way out of going to school again.

I was halfway across the room when I noticed Golden Lea's book, *Recollections*, on the night table, and I was instantly attracted. That's partly because I wanted to find out what happened next. But I was also starting to think that Mom and Gramma were right. Golden Lea could have accepted her fate. I mean, she ate and dressed a lot better than most of the other slaves, and she wasn't being worked half to death, either. But like Gramma said, Golden Lea wouldn't give up. There was something in her, some piece of her character, that couldn't accept being a slave. If that was her fate, she wasn't signing up for it.

I picked up the book and opened it. I was thinking that if I wasn't going to school, I'd have plenty of time to read. Maybe I could finish the whole thing before my biopsy tomorrow.

Sounds like a plan, right? Only when I looked at the handwriting, I couldn't read a single word. I could see the letters and the words just fine, but I couldn't read them. It was like the book was written in Polish or Chinese. I closed the book, shook my head back and forth, and opened it

75

again, thinking *puh-leeeze*, what now? I mean, seriously, gimme a break.

But nobody was listening. I felt shocked. And sad. And terrified. It was like I discovered something I shouldn't have, like when I was a kid and found Santa presents hidden in Mom and Dad's closet. Frantically, I began to turn the pages, pointing my finger at a particular word or letter, staring down until my eyes watered. All the while thinking, *My brain is getting worse. How am I gonna tell Mom?*

Then she walked into the room, and I just started crying.

Mom coped in her usual competent manner. She got on the phone and bullied her way from the hospital operator to Dr. Balder. Before he got on, I demanded that Mom switch over to the speakerphone. I wanted in on the conversation and listened anxiously, straining to hear every word over the frantic beating of my heart.

There weren't very many words. Mom described my new symptom, and Dr. Balder calmly instructed her to bring me to the hospital immediately. So we repeated the drive we'd taken the day before, along with all those millions of commuters. I was carrying my pink-and-yellow tie-dyed book bag, and I'd shoved Golden Lea's manuscript into it. Talk about dumb. I wanted to show Dr. Balder that I couldn't understand a word, but I didn't need the manuscript for that. I couldn't read *anything*.

And then I could.

Talk about weird. We were coming up on the George Washington Bridge and I glanced at a road sign and read, FORT LEE/ KEEP RIGHT. Then I read the signs coming across the bridge and the sign at the toll booths: E-Z PASS ONLY. To me, it was the most beautiful poetry I had ever read.

"I can read again!" I told my mother.

Of course, she responded with, "That's great, baby." But she didn't make a U-turn or even slow down, and I had the sense, though Dr. Balder hadn't said it, that some sort of line had been crossed. I was in it for keeps: No more watching. No more waiting. No more wishing it away.

When we got to the hospital, Dr. Balder was in surgery and it took an hour for us to be shown into his office. I expected him to be in a rush, but aside from a set of seriously offensive puke-green scrubs, he was as slow, steady, and direct as last time. And his tired eyes were just as kind.

But his message wasn't exactly what I wanted to hear. He told me that my inability to read was called aphasia and that it was caused by the mass effect of the tumor compressing my brain.

"Mass effects vary tremendously, depending on where a tumor is located. Your tumor is located in the part of your brain that processes language."

I remember thinking, *Okay, okay. That's not so bad. You have a little symptom, a little mass effect, and then it goes away. No big deal.*

But Dr. Balder wasn't having any. "My worry here," he continued, "is that sooner or later one of these episodes will prove to be permanent, especially coming one after the other as they have. I think we should operate immediately—today, later this afternoon—and remove as much of the tumor as possible. In my opinion, it's riskier to wait."

You know how those TV doctors always tell you to get a second opinion? Well, maybe somebody should clue them in about "mass effects" and "permanent neurological deficits" and how you better have an operation *right now* or your brain will melt and run out through your ears.

I didn't need another opinion. *My* opinion was that what Dr. Balder had already said was all I needed to hear. It was like a hard slap across the face.

I wanted this thing out of my body right away. I never asked for it and I didn't want it there. I didn't need it messing with my brain anymore, taking away my ability to walk, to read—and who knew what else was in store? Permanent damage? From this mass that had taken up residence in my head, like an uninvited houseguest, and was trying to take over my life? No. No way. That wasn't going to happen. Not if I still had any say-so in the matter.

I would do the surgery as soon as possible—this way, there was no time to think about it. But when Dr. Balder went on to describe the procedure and its risks, I found myself getting angry. I mean, this is what happened to that unlucky kid with her face on the jar at the corner drugstore: HELP THIS GIRL HAVE AN OPERATION. But I wasn't that girl. I couldn't be. I refused to see myself as some pitiful victim. I was the Montclair Flash, Maddie Bergamo, headed for college basketball, for the Olympics, for the pros. I had part of my life already mapped out and had been working toward my goals all along. Now, all of a sudden, there was a chance they would be lost—or *I* would.

I couldn't take any more. The doctor was going on about "probabilities" but we were dancing around the real issue. I balled my hands into fists and shouted, "If you think I'm gonna die, just say so." There. I had finally put my fear into words.

Mom's mouth dropped open, but Dr. Balder didn't skip a beat. "I don't think you're going to die, Maddie," he said. "It's a safe procedure with good results."

"So, I may just be a vegetable, right? Maddie, the turnip girl? Maybe I should find somebody to teach me sign language."

Mom reached out and put her arm around me before I could go on. That was the only thing that kept me from bursting into tears—a mixture of anger, sadness, fear, helplessness and that awful sense of unfairness welling up inside me. Because as Dr. Balder explained it, the operation, all by itself, could produce some of those permanent neurological deficits. I mean, talk about a crossfire. The miseries were coming at me from every direction. It was like having a ticking time bomb in my head: If I waited, it could go off on its own; if they tried to defuse it, any small misstep could cause it to explode.

And the description of the surgery didn't improve my confidence any. The biopsy had called for a hole the size of a dime; the craniotomy called for a hole the size of a saucer. A biopsy can be closed with a few stitches; the craniotomy would require enough stitches to sew a quilt.

By the time it was over, I felt like an animal trapped in a cage. Nowhere to hide, no escape, and no one riding to my rescue. And the worst part was that they took the cage and put it on a roller coaster. No fourteen-year-old should have to face the immediate possibility of death or disability… and here I was, hurtling toward it at full speed.

The admitting procedure came first. Mom and I filled out enough forms to stuff a file cabinet before I was taken upstairs to a room with two beds inside, neither currently occupied. I was numb when I walked into it. Not just my leg. My entire body.

Additional testing followed: more blood ("Just a little pinch, dear"), more urine, another EEG, a chest X-ray. The nurses were cheery, of course, but I was back to thinking of myself as a machine and the medical personnel as mechanics checking my various parts.

"Oh my goodness, her electrical system is really out of whack," I imagined them saying the second they left the room.

But that wasn't the worst of it. Dr. Balder had decided on stereotactic surgery. When he first said that word—stereotactic—I thought, *Okay, how bad can it be?* Stereos are good things. I have one in my bedroom. Well, "bad" isn't the right word. "Dehumanizing" would be a lot better.

The point of stereotactic surgery is to guide the surgeon to the exact spot of the tumor, sparing the brain tissue itself. So, an MRI is taken to pinpoint the tumor, then an aluminum frame is *pinned* to your head. Think of it as having braces and headgear—only a thousand times scarier.

I mean, does that sound painful, or what? Well, the actual pinning part doesn't hurt. No, the pain part comes when they numb your head where the pins are attached.

"Just a little pinch, dear."

But they weren't little, and they didn't pinch. They burned like somebody stuck a match under my scalp. And when they attached the pins, it felt like my skull was about to cave in from the weight.

"Try not to move your head, dear. We don't want to alter the coordinates." Alter the coordinates?! Isn't that how Columbus found America? Exactly what were they looking for in there?

Did I mention that a nurse shaved the side of my head before they attached the frame? Horrible. Did I mention that they washed the hair I had left and painted my scalp orangey-red with antiseptic? Freakish. Did I mention that a parade of doctors came into my room to ask me the same questions over and over? Frustrating. Oh, and did I mention that when Mom saw me wearing the frame, she gasped and put her hand to her mouth? Absolutely devastating.

Yeah, that last one was a good one. Fear wasn't real big on Mom's psychological agenda, but now she was petrified. And me? They don't have a word to describe how scared I was. Not even on the SATs.

As I lay on the bed, having what can only be described as an out-of-body experience, every nurse and every doctor who came waltzing into the room delivered the same message—which was especially emphatic from one doctor with a complexion so gray he might have been dug out of a grave. His name was Dr. Shevosky and he was a radiation oncologist.

"Pleeze sit still. Vee do not vant to move," he instructed me in a heavy accent. "Ozzervise, vee might accidentally remove your ear."

I don't know. Maybe I don't have a sense of humor, because I didn't even break a smile. In fact, what I wanted to do was take off the frame and smack him with it. And I might have done it, too, if the frame wasn't pinned to my skull.

I was angry. To put it mildly. And I'd been angry since I woke up and found that I couldn't read. I mean, the stark reality was that Dr. Balder was going to cut my head open and he couldn't even promise to remove the whole tumor… and maybe he'd do more harm than good to my brain.

Can you say, *Puh-leeeze?* Can you say, *Gimme a break?* Can you say, *What did I do to deserve this?*

I had every right to be angry. And scared. And terrified. Those emotions were the only things keeping me from becoming an aluminum-headed robot. I think I went through the entire spectrum of human emotions during those few hours.

Then, somewhere around four o'clock, they put me on a gurney and wheeled me off to the operating room. That's when my dad showed up. He took one look at me, his face reddened, and he burst into tears.

"Phillip," Mom said in that voice she uses when she wants to catch your attention.

I don't know which was worse: Daddy crying, or Mom shutting him down. I understand she was just trying to have everyone put on a brave face for my sake. But being that I couldn't cry—mostly because a nurse had given me something to "calm me down" a half-hour before and I was as limp as an overcooked strand of fettuccini—there was something *normal* about my father's tears. Something I couldn't express myself. It was oddly reassuring.

Both my parents kissed me at the elevator, which was as far as they were allowed to go. It was like getting ready to board an airplane, which I did for the first time by myself last summer when I went to visit my cousins in Georgia. My parents couldn't come with me to the terminal gates. So, from there, I was on my own.

They both told me that they loved me. I whispered that I loved them, too, and then the elevator door opened and I was gone.

Not that I was alone. I was with some nameless and faceless hospital staff that I thought of as "them." They took me downstairs to the operating suite and left me in a corridor while they prepared the room. I was covered by a thin hospital blanket that didn't come close to keeping me warm, especially now with half my head shaved.

Naturally, I tried to get someone's attention—to get another blanket or just find out what was going to happen next—but I was groggy, and the operating room personnel were moving too fast. So I just lay there and shivered until my gurney was pushed into the operating room and I saw the glaring lights over the table and the gleaming instruments all laid out. Then I felt more alone than I ever had in my life.

Of course, "they" were all around me then, too. With surgical masks and plastic gloves. But believe me when I tell you that I felt I was all alone.

I don't remember much about the operation—which is how it should be, I suppose. The anesthesiologist put me to sleep with a small needle, making me count backwards from ten, like the clock running down at the end of one of my basketball games. Ten, nine, eight, seven... I don't remember how far I made it, though I do recall expecting the game-ending buzzer to go off. I probably even wondered if we won.

I was unconscious when Dr. Balder opened my scalp and cut away a chunk of my skull. Later on, after the tumor was exposed, I was brought up to some sort of awareness. I vaguely remember being asked a series of questions, but I can't recall them or what I answered.

Throughout the process, I didn't experience any discomfort. Dr. Balder had told me that the brain doesn't feel pain and he was right. With my scalp numbed up, I didn't feel anything, even though a piece of my skull was sitting in a dish next to the operating table. I didn't look at it because I couldn't turn my head. I wouldn't have wanted to see it, anyway. But I was vaguely aware of it through my peripheral vision, just as I was aware of Dr. Balder working away at the top of my head.

From the operating room, I went to the intensive care unit and back to being unconscious. Mom was holding my hand and Daddy was standing at the foot of the bed when I woke up an hour later. My father is a very neat man. Mom even kids him about it sometimes. But he didn't look neat at that moment. His hair was mussed, and he hadn't shaved, and his shirt was partially untucked. But—grungy or not—boy, was I glad to see him!

He looked so worried, though, and I wanted to cheer him up—him and Mom, too. But Dr. Balder had added a painkiller, Demerol, to the mix of drugs running through my system and I could barely raise my hand. I could speak, though, and I asked my mom to show me something I could read. She fished a paperback novel out of her purse and held it up. I was relieved when I recognized the title and the author's name, then fell back on the pillow and went to sleep again, happy for the little things in life, like being able to read, and happy for the big things, like family.

And, of course, for life itself. My hair, I figured, would grow back.

The next morning, I was taken from the intensive care unit back to my room. I felt okay. I mean, at least everything was working. Mom and Dad were still with me, looking pretty pleased with my progress—or at least their acting skills had improved—and Dr. Balder seemed unworried when he came into the room. Which is not to say that he brought good news.

By then, I was on Demerol for pain, Zofran for nausea, Pepcid for stomach acid, and Heparin to thin my blood. This was in addition to the Dilantin, the steroid, and the antibiotic I was already taking. I didn't know what was a side effect of which meds, or an effect of the surgery, or a symptom of my tumor. I only knew that my head was spinning like the wind-up ballerina on the music box in my bedroom. That made it hard to concentrate, but I did my best.

"First the good news."

Dr. Balder's smile was too tight and I was pretty sure, despite my confusion, that the good news wouldn't be good enough. Uh-uh. This game was far from over.

"We removed almost all of the tumor without doing any damage to the surrounding tissue," he continued. "The tumor is ninety-five percent smaller than it was. That should go a long way toward easing the mass effect."

Dr. Balder was staring directly into my eyes. I don't exactly know what he was looking for, but he couldn't have seen much. I could barely focus.

"We did an EEG last night," he said. "I think you slept through the whole thing, so you probably don't remember. Anyway, the results are good. You know the old saw about the physician's oath: First of all, do no harm. In that, we succeeded admirably."

Admirably? Now I was thinking, *Hey, all right. Now let's hear the bad news.* Before I fall asleep again.

"Of course, leaving any part of a tumor in place, even a few cells, can result in the tumor growing again. We won't be able to deal with that end of the equation until the pathology report comes back and we know exactly what we're dealing with. Some tumors grow rapidly, others very slowly."

"And how long will that take?" Mom asked. "For the report to be completed?"

"Twenty-four hours, give or take." Dr. Balder's thin smile widened just a bit. "Then we'll have to consider the various possibilities. Chemotherapy or radiation, or a combination of the two. Or possibly returning to a watch-and-wait approach." Finally, he turned back to me. "This isn't the time to worry, Maddie. Now is when you rest and recover your strength. If all goes well, and I expect it to, you'll be home in a couple of days."

Home. Just the word sounded amazing.

When Dr. Balder left a few minutes later, I slowly touched the bandage on the side of my head, moving my finger from one little bump to another. The little bumps were stitches, and there were too many to count.

My mom was holding my hand at that point and I pulled her a little closer. "I want to see myself in the mirror," I said, swallowing hard. "The one in your purse."

Naturally, Mom was all, *Oh, baby is this the right time?* But I didn't have the energy to argue and I started to reach for her bag. That got her moving. She rummaged around for a minute, then brought out her compact and opened it.

When I pulled off one side of the bandage, I expected to see the worst. I expected to see the worst and I wanted to get it over with. I wasn't disappointed. What I saw was almost more than I could handle: a crescent of tiny stitches—fifty-five, I found out later—traced a line through my shaved scalp, from above my eye to behind my ear.

I looked hideous and, for a second, I felt the hot sting of tears forming in my eyes. Then I realized that even though I wasn't much to look at for the time being, at least I could see. And move my hands. And hold a mirror.

But then I imagined myself going back to school in a few weeks. Yeah, that'd be great. Maybe I could dye what hair I had left ink-black and claim I was going Goth. Or have the Bengali Rose pick up some crazy scarves for me in the vintage shops and use them to cover my head—you know, try to start a new trend. Or maybe I'd just be a freak, the girl with the hole in her head. One thing was sure: I was too tall to hide, so that wasn't an option. And even if I were shorter, I'm not sure how much I'd like the idea of hiding who I am anyway.

Finally, I replaced the bandage, thinking that maybe Dr. Balder was right. I should take it one day at a time. Rest and recover, then face whatever comes next.

"Mom?"

"Yes, honey?" she said, putting away the mirror.

"Where did you put my book bag? I remember putting Golden Lea's book in it before we left home."

I thought I detected Mom's lips curl slightly into a frown. I'm sure she didn't want the manuscript leaving the house, but you couldn't really scold a kid who just had a brain tumor removed, now could you?

"Just a minute," she said in her more pleasant tone. "Your bag is right beside the bed." She leaned over for a moment, then came up with the book.

"I want you to read it to me," I said in a weak voice. "I'd read it myself, but I just don't have the strength to hold it up."

And what was Mom gonna say to that? No?

True, she gave me a suspicious look—and I was laying it on a little thick—but I think she was relieved. If I was sharp enough to manipulate her, maybe everything would be all right after all.

What can I say? I wanted to hear my mom's voice. To know she was right there as I closed my eyes and listened to the words wash over me. Mom usually loved reading to me. It was something we'd done together since I was a little kid.

But what she didn't particularly care for was Golden Lea's dialect. It's one thing for a black woman to read that dialect, another thing to speak the words out loud. But Mom was always a trooper and after a minute of stumbling over the words, she settled into the story.

Chapter 7

NEVER LOSE HOPE

*M*Y PA, ELIJAH, *God rest his soul, was a quiet man.*
That's mos likely why he had that way of his with
horses. I seen many a man talk to horses, talk to em like they
was peoples. What I reckon is they was scared of horses and
they wanted to make a horse into a person. Pa, he talked to
the horses by jus bein there. I seen it many a time, but this
particular time struck me powerful hard. One of Masta's prize
thorobred stallions kicked a stable boy to the floor of the barn
and went on a rampage. Lands, that horse's eyes was rollin
all in his head like he was havin some kinda fit, and he was
kickin and bitin at anyone come near him. And the worse
part was that Masta wouldn't do nothin to that stallion if he
broke every bone in the boy's body. But he'd be right unhappy
if that horse got hurt.

Me, I ran up the ladder into the hayloft real quick, but Pa
wasn't put out a'tall. No, sir. He came up on the animal real
slow and took the bridle. Then he stroked the horse's muzzle,
all the time noddin his head. The horse did rear up once, but

then he settled down fine and Pa led him to his stall like he weren't no more trouble than a ol plow horse.

Pa was like that in everything he did. Slow and quiet, thinkin all the time. He knowed if we was to escape, we had to do somethin bout them bloodhounds. There weren't no way we could outrun em, not unless we grew wings and flew away. Mos folks woulda gave up, but Pa jus figured on the problem till he found an answer.

It was Saturday evenin, and we was in his little cabin, eatin buttermilk biscuits that I toted from the kitchen, when he tole me what he had in mind.

"Masta Harris in Virginia," Pa said, "but he comin back to Louisville by the railroad in two days time. And Tom, like he always do, gonna take the coach and fetch Masta home. Now, Louisville is forty miles away and if Tom wants to git there on time, he gotta leave fore sunrise. And what we gonna do is hide ourselfs in the luggage box on Masta's coach till Tom gits away from Belle Maison. Then we take to the woods."

Now, I already said that escapin weren't no little thing. Yes, sir, I was all for it when we was jus talkin, but now that we was bout to do the deed, I gotta admit that I was mighty scared. I was thinkin that gettin switched hurt somethin awful, so whippin mus be a whole lot worse. And it weren't like I never seen nobody whipped.

"What's Tom gonna say when he see us, Pa?"

Pa laughed. "I spect he's gonna be right surprised. But he ain't gonna say nothin a'tall."

"Why's that?"

"Two reasons, Golden Lea. First, Tom's a Christian man. Second, if he opens his mouth, Masta gonna think he helped us. Don't matter that we fooled Tom. Masta got his own way of

figurin and it's mosly that slaves is always plannin some kinda devilment. Tom knows this like he knows his own name. Bes thing he can do is go right on to Louisville like ain't nothin happened. And that's jus what he gonna do."

Pa's plan went a long way toward soothin my nerves. Which ain't to say that I wasn't still scared. But Pa took his plan one step further. Night fore we left Belle Maison, he slipped out and ran back and forth to a swamp bout two miles to the east. He was figurin them dogs would pick up that trail and lead Masta in the direction opposite of where we was goin. Then Masta would search that swamp for days while we headed north to Ohio.

The night we left was the longest night I ever passed. Missy Ann, she fell asleep the minute her head touched that feather pillow. And like always, she lay there like a body stretched out on the coolin board. Didn't hardly move a inch. But I was still checkin her every other minute to be sure, which only made me all the more nervous. I swear, when I finally picked up the Bible jus fore I slipped out the room, my heart was beatin so fast I thought I was gonna burst.

And things didn't git no better on that hallway and down them stairs. Course, there was only Mistriss Sarah and Winnie in the family wing of Belle Maison, but I felt their eyes on me with every tippy-toe step I took. And when them stairs creaked, I figured I was for sho caught. I was spectin Mistriss Sarah to come flyin down the stairs after me. But weren't nobody comin, nobody watchin, ceptin for the Masta's two spaniels. They walked right up and sniffs my feet, scarin me mos half to death. But them dogs knowed me good and they jus turned round and trotted off.

Well, I crossed that yard to the barn so fast I thought for a minute that I done growed me some wings. I flied right into my pa's arms. And I guess I musta been part horse, cause he calmed me down without sayin nary a word. Jus held me there till my heart slowed down and I could breathe again. Then we hid ourselfs out in the luggage box.

That luggage box was mighty big on accounta Mistriss Sarah liked to travel in style and there weren't enough room on top of the carriage to tie her things down. So Masta had the carpenters build a wooden box and fasten it to the back of the carriage.

Me and Pa, we was able to sit cramped up with our backs against opposite ends of the box and our feet touchin. We had a sack filled with food and a patchwork blanket and other necessities, like a knife and rope enough to make a snare. I didn't reckon we'd need the blanket, bein as it was high summer and we was gonna walk at night and rest durin the day. But then I didn't knowed nothin bout where we was goin. Didn't knowed if there was mountains or rivers or I might walk off the end of the world. I jus knowed we was goin and there was no turnin back.

We was in the luggage box for near three hours fore Tom hitched up the horses and headed down the road to Louisville. That road, it was dirt and the ruts in it run deep. Me and Pa was bounced around, bangin our knees and our heads, but we didn't stir till we was far away from Belle Maison. Then we opened the top of the luggage box and jumped up like a coupla ghosts.

Ol Tom didn't so much as shiver. He jus turned round and look at us. Then he said, "I been wondrin who was layin up in the box."

"How you know somebody was in there?" I asked.

"Golden Lea, I knows this carriage like your pa knows horses. First thing, when I come out this mornin, I sees the carriage was hangin too low in back."

"How come you didn't do nothin?"

"Well, I figured it was Marcellus. He got a wife lives on a farm outside Louisville. Marcellus don't git to see her and them kids very often."

"Well, it ain't Marcellus," Pa said. "It's me and Golden Lea. We goin north to Ohio."

"I been to Ohio once, with Masta. Drove him up to a place called Cincinnati."

"I hear there's a river gotta be crossed."

"The Ohio River. We come across it on a ferry boat. But the river ain't the only problem you got. And you ain't the only slaves ever run away north. There's slave catchers on both side of that river, lots of em. Shoot you, soon as look at you."

Pa jumped down off the carriage and then helped me down. "Be that as it may, Tom, there ain't no turnin back now. We already been missed."

"Well, then," Tom said, "I hope the Lord is smilin down on you this day. Cause you gonna need all the help you can git."

We didn't walk no more than a mile into the forest fore we settled down. Travelin by day was jus too dangerous. Course, travelin by night weren't exactly safe, neither, not on the roads. Them patrollers rode out mos every night. So our plan was to travel after dark, usin the North Star to guide us, and stick to them woods.

Funny thing bout that North Star. Masta Harris did everythin he could to make sure his slaves was ignorant, but *the slaves on his plantation all knowed how to find the North Star, includin me. Over the years, I looked up at that guidin star many a time, dreamin of my freedom. And I spects that mos every slave on every plantation, even way down south, done the same thing. Masta, he woulda never believed that his slaves was thinkin bout freedom. No, he was always tellin his guests, specially them as come from the north, that his slaves was happy. But the only things Masta Harris knowed bout his slaves was how to work em. What they felt? What they thought? Bout them things he was ignorant as the mice in his barn.*

We laid up for the day on a patch of logged-over land. The trees was jus comin back, red maples for the mos part, and they was growin tight together. We pushed into em till we found a clearin big enough to lay the blanket down then settled in. Us and the gnats and the skeeters and the flies and the summer heat.

We was sposed to rest, since we been walkin all night. But we was way too excited and I didn't fall asleep till the sun passed overhead. Pa woke me up in the late afternoon. I didn't know where I was for a minute. The shade was deep but low down over my head, and the sun was shinin behind the leaves. I felt like I was inside a green tent.

There weren't much to the meal that me and Pa ate. Pa had managed to git a good piece of ham from the smokehouse—I never did find out how he done it—and we had a little sack full of cornbread and biscuits and another sack filled with dried up apples from last year. Not much, I gotta admit. But we only had to go bout seventy miles. Leastwise, iffen I calculated right. Missy Ann's geography book had a little line on the bottom, say, One inch equals fifteen miles. I measured that line with a string and laid the string down tween where I figured Belle

Maison was and the Ohio River. That's how I come to arrive on seventy miles. Only I knowed, even as I sat on that blanket, chewin on one of them apples, that I might be all wrong. I had never paid much attention to geography fore and my numbers wasn't that good, neither.

See, we was relyin on my calculatin, so we only brought food enough for three days. Pa wanted to travel light on accounta he had to carry everything on his back. Well, as things come out, my reckonin was pretty true. It's near bout seventy miles from Clark County to the Ohio River. But there's miles on a road and there's miles through a forest and they ain't no ways the same.

We started out as soon as it got dark and right away I could see we was in trouble. There was fallen trees to cut around and low limbs that whipped at our bodies and faces, and the skeeters—when they wasn't bitin us—was buzzin all round our heads. Mos of the time, we couldn't see the North Star, or any stars a'tall, through the branches of the trees. Then we come to a swamp where I heard the wolves.

Ain't no one knows why a wolf howls. Maybe they singin bout pretty gals they once courted, or bout how they misses their mamas. Or maybe they singin to the Lord in some kinda animal way. I ain't no wolf and I can't say. But I do know there ain't no lonelier sound in all the world than the howl of a wolf. No, sir. To me, that night, it sounded like them wolves was cryin for all the lost souls in this world. And me, Golden Lea Jackson, fourteen-year-old slave girl, was surely the mos lost of em all.

There was times that first night I thought dawn would never come. I was bruised and cut and itchin from a hundred bites and so tired from fightin the brambles and the logs that my legs was like rubber. But that weren't the worst. No, the worst was that we mos likely hadn't come more than ten miles and mos of that was movin east or west to git around obstacles. And those obstacles wasn't only swamps and such. Twice we come across farms and we was mighty tempted to cut through them fields. But every farmer kep dogs and if they catched our smell and started barkin, the farmer would surely come out to check on his livestock. So all we could do was stop for a few seconds to sight the North Star and then move right back into the darkness of the forest.

But we done the bes we could, me and Pa, and we didn't cry bout it, neither. Come mornin, jus fore it started to rain, we found a space beneath a rocky outcropping at the crest of a hill and had ourselfs a little to eat. Then me and Pa wound the blanket round us and huddled together. Natrally, we couldn't build us no fire—no more than we could cross them farmers' fields—and we was mighty discouraged. Even our breakfast was skimpy cause we only took food for three days and Ohio was gettin further and further away.

I could see Pa was feelin right low and I spect he was guilty bout draggin me into this here trouble. I wanted to raise his spirits and I only knowed one way to do it. I opened the Bible to the book of Exodus, chapter 3, and started readin out loud. We was sittin way back in the shadows and I had to draw the Holy Book real close, but I puzzled out the words all right.

But the Lord said, I have witnessed the affliction of my peoples and have heard their cry of complaint against the slave drivers, so I knowed well what they is sufferin. Therefore I have come down to rescue them and lead them outta that land to a good and spacious land, a land of milk and honey.

I read on for maybe another hour, bout the trials and tribulation of Moses and the Israelites, till I was too tired to go on and I fell asleep. When I woke up, my bones was sore from sleepin on them rocks, but there weren't nothin to do but go on. And there wasn't nothin changed, ceptin that twice we come upon roads, one of em headin north. We was mighty tempted to take that north road, but white folks don't build roads for escapin slaves. They builds em to connect farms and towns, so we jus crossed over and continued on. It's a good thing we did, too, cause we didn't git no more than a hundred feet into the forest when we heard the hoof beats. And it weren't no elk this time. These was patrollers, dressed up in them long gray coats, and if we have been on that road, we woulda been caught for sure.

"Lord help us," my pa said after they was gone.

I wasn't brought up to sass my pa and I didn't say nothin. But the way I figured, the Lord had already helped us plenty, and if we had faith, He would help us again. Fact, I was right smug bout it. That's cause some of the Lord's strange ways was as yet unknown to me.

We come down a hill jus fore sunrise, to a creek that ran through a narrow valley, and we stopped to drink. I rememba them birds was singin up a storm and there was a steady breeze blowin through the river birch hangin over the water. Pa laid down his sack and bent down over the creek, reachin down to fill a small jug, and I jus dropped down beside him. That was when we heard that click. Ain't nothin in nature makes a sound like that, but we both knowed what it was. The click of a hammer drawn back, the hammer on a gun, and it's bout the mos chillin sound I knowed. But it weren't no more chillin than the words that followed.

"Now don't y'all make me have to go and shoot ya. Be a plumb waste of ammunition."

Chapter 8

SOURCES OF STRENGTH

M Y MOM WAS the fuel that powered the Bergamo family ship. She was a ball of energy, always in the process of implementing some plan or other. This was why she'd been selected to supervise the trial division at the department of finance. Keeping fifteen balls in the air at the same time was her specialty. I think any other man besides my dad would have found her impossible to live with.

If Mom was the fuel that drove the ship, Daddy was the rudder that steered the ship away from the rocks. Steady as she goes—that must have been his motto. He never got excited and moving him off-course was not an option. Most likely, that's why he was chosen to deliver a lecture the day after my surgery.

But he was here now, when I woke up, and Mom was nowhere to be found.

"Where's Mom?" I asked groggily, recalling the last section of Golden Lea's memoirs that she had been reading to me. I really wanted to hear more, and I couldn't believe that I fell asleep at such an exciting part.

It was the meds. It had to be. Normally, I'd stay up forever with a book I liked. Nothing could get me to put it down: not the fact that school was starting in a few short hours, or that my eyes would look so red and puffy the next morning that I'd have to make up a new allergy just so my mother wouldn't know I was reading all night. That's how I lost my goose-down comforter last year when the new Toni Morrison novel came out. Oh, well. We switched to "down alternative," which was almost just as warm and probably better for the geese.

"Your mother's on a food run to the cafeteria," my dad said. Poor things. Because they refused to leave my side, they'd been stuck eating hospital food, too. That's love for you.

"Oh," I said. "When she comes back, I'm going to ask her to read to me some more."

I could see my father's expression change. "Uh, Maddie…" he began. "I don't want to make you feel bad, but your mother's a little upset." He said it in a soothing voice, but I could tell that something was weighing heavily on his mind.

"Gee, why is that, Daddy?" In fact, I had no idea.

My father steepled his fingers and leaned forward in his chair. "Golden Lea's manuscript is a precious relic in your mom's family, all the more so because it's extremely fragile. She didn't want to say anything, but you jamming it into your book bag and bringing it here to the hospital upset her."

"I thought there were copies," I said. Then I saw the look on Daddy's face and I knew I wasn't getting away with that one. Nobody thinks a copy of the Mona Lisa, no matter how perfect, is equal to the original.

"I don't know what I was thinking," I admitted. "I was like, omigosh, I can't read. Everything else just kinda happened."

"It's all right, honey. She's not mad at you, but I'm afraid you won't be seeing—or hearing—the rest of the story until you get home."

I understood. Besides, I didn't have the energy to argue, but I really wanted to find out what came next. The howling of the wolves seemed very real to me. A few years before, I'd gone to a wilderness camp in the Adirondack Mountains. Camp Iroquois was like, *puh-leeeze*, do I look like a pioneer? But I remember a group of us being taken for a night walk through the woods. The two camp counselors in charge had flashlights, but during one section of the hike, they turned the lights off and we marched on, guided only by a sliver of moonlight. Talk about creepy. I wasn't just afraid of the creatures that might be out there—the bears and the bats and the rattlesnakes. No, I was thinking werewolves and vampires.

So, if I was scared then, how did Golden Lea feel as she forced her way through the briars and brambles? Knowing that any minute she might be taken? And, worse than the wolves, the last thing she heard was a gun click. I don't even *know* what that sounds like in real life.

Golden Lea was only fourteen, and even with her father by her side, she must have felt pretty alone and vulnerable. Like I did when I went into surgery.

As it turned out, I didn't have a lot of time to consider the issue of how Golden Lea felt—not then, anyway. Mom arrived a few minutes later, with a tray of cafeteria food and Dr. Balder following behind like he was being towed in her wake.

"Good afternoon, Maddie," he said. "How are you feeling?"

This was like the two-hundredth time I'd been asked the same question that day. Mom had asked it a hundred times all by herself. But I answered politely.

"I'm very tired."

"Well, that's natural."

I sensed that he wanted to let it go right there, but I wasn't finished. "I want to stop taking the Demerol. It's making me fog out. I mean, sometimes I don't even know what I'm feeling." And I suspected that was the drug that made me fall asleep at the exciting part of the book.

"That's a fine idea. I'll instruct the nursing staff not to bring it unless you ask. And we'll cancel the Pepcid, too, now that you're eating."

I frowned, thinking of the beef broth and orange Jell-O served for lunch. Yes, I managed to get the mess into my stomach. That was because I knew I'd never get anything else to eat if I didn't. But I wouldn't exactly call it "eating." I'd call it "trying to survive and not starve to death."

"Anyway," Dr. Balder continued, "I have some extremely good news."

"And bad news?" I asked. I was pretty wise to his game by now.

"No, not this time," he smiled. "The pathology report is in. Your tumor is called a juvenile pilocytic astrocytoma. It's not malignant, it didn't come from some other part of your body, and it's extremely slow-growing." He paused to look at each of us in turn. Me first, then Mom, then my dad. "Really, it's great news. I couldn't be happier."

It was like Dr. Balder waved a magic wand. *Everybody* teared up, except for me. My reaction was entirely physical. The tension just drained away, leaving me feeling as stale as the burnt toast Mom put out for the birds. But in a good way. Like a *peaceful* piece of toast.

Mom held out as long as she could before asking a question…which was, like, less than ten seconds. "What about therapy?" she asked. "Will she still need…treatment?"

Dr. Balder nodded once, smiled his kind-doctor smile, then spoke directly to me. "Fortunately, there's no rush here, but I'll outline the possibilities. Pilocytic astrocytomas are truly slow-growing. You might go the rest of your life without experiencing another symptom. On the other hand, through a combination of radiation and chemotherapy, we could even improve those odds and the tumor might be completely eliminated for good. I won't minimize the effects of these therapies. We've made any number of improvements over the years, but the regimen is still grueling."

"I'll lose my hair, right?" I asked.

"Most of it, yes. But your hair will grow back."

"Well, I guess it's not looking all that great these days anyway. Might as well start all over with a clean slate."

The doctor smiled again. "There are other effects as well. But this is not the time to talk about them. If no problems develop overnight, you'll be going home tomorrow. In a week, when you come back to have the stitches removed, I'll have an oncologist there to discuss your options."

Naturally, Mom wasn't satisfied. She peppered Dr. Balder with questions. I think she wanted him to lay down the odds. Six-to-one if we watch and wait. Four-to-one if we do radiation alone. Three-to-one if we do radiation and chemo. But Dr. Balder didn't have a crystal ball and he wasn't in the psychic business.

"You're right, Mrs. Moore-Bergamo," Dr. Balder said patiently when my mom finally stopped for air. "Neither chemotherapy nor radiation offers any guarantee. Some tumor cells may survive, and the radiation, by itself, can do long-term damage. But, of course, we know we didn't completely eliminate the tumor with the surgery. If there was any chance that we had, we wouldn't be talking about these options now."

Okay, so there was some bad news. But it was a matter of keeping the tumor from coming back—and that was something I could *definitely* get on board with.

Like Dr. Balder had promised, I did get to go home on the following day. Checking out of the hospital was one of the best feelings of my life, though I knew it was just a reprieve. I couldn't wait to get off of the hospital "sickness schedule"—breakfast at eight o'clock, nurse checks your temperature at nine o'clock, next nurse comes in to check your bandages at ten o'clock, etc., etc.—and was looking forward to things getting back to "normal." Even though it was a new type of "normal" that I'd need to get used to, I could get there at my own pace…and there wouldn't be anymore Jell-O!

The ride home was smooth and I was really enjoying my freedom and the fresh air that didn't smell like antiseptic. In fact, I was loving all of it—until we got to Montclair. Then I scrunched way down in my seat. That's because I didn't want anyone from school seeing me, not yet. Half of my head was covered by a thick bandage and my scalp was sore and itchy at the edges of the wound. Plus, I had a headache that bordered on filthy. It wasn't exactly my finest hour. I mean, after this, I'll never again worry about how I look when I get a zit.

Now that I'd cut out the Demerol, my thinking was a lot sharper. Which meant I'd be heading back to school, and sooner rather than later. Which also meant I had to come up with a plan, fast.

I was thinking I'd get one of those retro hats: a cloche, like the kind worn by the flappers in the 1920s. Some of those hats pull down to cover the ears. Jasmine the Bengali Rose might have some ideas—in fact, it would give her another excuse to go shopping. As if she needed one. Maybe I'd decorate it with political campaign pins from my dad's collection. Daddy had pins going back to the late nineteenth century, but I wasn't exactly sure he'd lend them to me. Dad, like, never sold his pins. He only bought more, which did not endear him to Mom, not since he commandeered one of the back bedrooms to display his collection. But I figured if I looked pitiful enough, he'd probably go along.

I mean, I had to do *something*, right? Middle school is not the time or the place to get behind the curve or to start acting all insecure. No, I was going to have to front, big time. In-your-face was definitely the order of the day. Or at least on the day I went back to school. It was only a matter of coming up with a suitable strategy.

For the time being, though, I was anything but in-your-face. I was more like hide-your-face and crouch down low in the car. Like those kids who slouch behind their desks in the back of the classroom when they haven't read the homework material, hoping to make themselves invisible so the teacher won't call on them. Well, it didn't usually work for them. But it worked wonders for me.

My mom caught what I was doing out of the corner of her eye while she was driving, but thankfully she didn't call me out on it. She let me keep up my bad posture all the way to our front driveway. I made it home without being recognized. Now, all I had to do was make it into the house.

I turned the collar of my jacket up high and tucked my head in like a turtle. If I had big sunglasses, I would've put them on, too, and looked like any number of celebrities trying to get past the paparazzi. Only I don't think anyone would've wanted to take my picture. As quickly as possible, I made it out of the car and into my house.

Ahhh, home… Generally, teenagers try to spend as much time as possible out of their houses. We kill time at the mall with classmates, or take turns sleeping over at our best friends' places. We feel like losers if we spend a Friday night at home, and our least favorite punishment is getting grounded. But, let me tell you this: When I walked into my house, I realized that there was nowhere else on earth I'd rather be. Not to sound corny or too much like Dorothy, but there really is no place like home. *Especially* after spending so much time in the hospital.

So, what did I do when I got home? I smelled the non-hospital-smelling air. I looked at the non-hospital-colored walls. I checked the refrigerator for any signs of Jell-O. None. I waited for a few minutes to see if "they"—random nurses, miscellaneous doctors—would come walking into the room unannounced to take my blood or check my bandages. Nothing. Satisfied, I smiled, struggled to stay up for a little while, then went upstairs to bed.

Even though I expected to be feeling better *out* of the hospital, I was still really tired. When mom took my temperature, I didn't have a fever. Still, I fell asleep within a few minutes.

Three hours later, when I woke up *in my own bed*—down-alternative comforter and all—I could hear someone's voice downstairs. I recognized it immediately. It was Marsha, chatting away with my mom and dad.

Marsha Pierce, a.k.a. Marsha the Nerd, was one of the Mag-7s and my BFF since we met in second grade. To her, nerdism was a spiritual path, like Zen or yoga. It was her way of announcing to the world (or at least to the other kids in middle school) that it's *what* you know, not *who* you know, that's important, and it's not how you look, but how you look at the world that defines you.

There was only one problem with all of that: Marsha wasn't naturally nerdy. So to rectify that, she underwent an image overhaul of her own to make herself *less* noticeable and *more* nerd-like. Her hair was a natural honey-brown, but she not only dyed it mousy-brown, she parted it right down the middle and let it fall in a ragged line midway between her ears and her shoulders. Add to that a pair of oversized cat-eye glasses and a retainer that she kept on wearing years after her teeth were perfectly straight, and you have the public Marsha Pierce: fearless in her choices, untouched by middle school fashion and immune to the usual cliquey melodrama. For the most part, she was happy to fly under the radar.

The private Marsha was another story. At home, she had an absent father and an alcoholic mother, and actually *wanted* their attention. I think the nerd-dom was a type of armor she used that made it okay for her to feel ignored by her parents, because she was used to it from her peers. But there was only one problem with that, too. As soon as Marsha opened her mouth, she was impossible to ignore.

She was the smartest kid in the school, maybe the smartest kid in the state. Come next fall, she'd be headed off to The Choate School on a full scholarship. Aside from being John F. Kennedy's alma mater, The Choate School is a gateway to Harvard. The tuition for boarding students runs more than forty grand a year. She'd be a nerd among preppies with "perfect" lives and "perfect" families. And I was sure she'd get her message across there, too. Which is why, despite the frightful way I looked, I knew I wouldn't have to worry about Marsha judging me. So I took a deep breath—and a quick look in the bathroom mirror—and went downstairs to see her.

When she first saw me, Marsha was in the middle of a sentence, which she didn't finish. Her mouth sort of hung open for a few seconds with no words coming out and her eyes widened slightly, but she recovered quickly.

She stood up from the table, took a few quick steps my way and hugged me. It was sweet—but weird. Marsha and I weren't what you'd call the affectionate types. We weren't the kind of girls who hugged each other good-bye when lunch ended, even though they'd see each other after school, or the ones who jumped up and down squealing in a high-pitched, dog whistle kind of way whenever they got the least bit of good news.

But Marsha's hug meant a lot to me just then. I felt like I was being accepted back into "normal" society.

"How are you feeling?" Marsha asked, her voice full of concern. See? She went right past the appearance and got to the heart of the matter: how I was on the inside.

"I'm okay," I said, though honestly I wasn't. I had awakened with a slight headache and felt like I could have slept another three hours, easily.

She filled me in on what was happening at school, which really wasn't that much but seemed incredibly interesting to me at the moment since I was pretty starved for social contact and news from the non-sick outside world. Not that she had any "insider information," like whether or not Jason Walker had a date for the dance. But she told me about what I was missing in math class and other nerd-related news.

"All the Mag-7s miss you, you know," she said with a smile. It made me feel better than all the medicine in the world.

Marsha didn't stay long, which was good, in a way. Well, three ways. First of all, she didn't look all that comfortable, which wasn't exactly something I expected. I imagine it's hard to see your best friend go through something like this and know what to say—and it wasn't my intention to get pity or make anyone feel strange around me.

Second, I wasn't feeling all that talkative. I didn't want to answer too many questions about my illness—the jinx was part of it, but I was also getting tired of focusing on myself and spending most of my time thinking about all the details of the sickness and maintenance routine.

Third, I didn't feel so great myself. I seemed to be getting more tired by the minute and the mild headache I had was becoming more intense.

When Marsha left, I went back upstairs and slept right through dinner, then woke up at ten o'clock with a fever of 100.8 degrees. By midnight, my fever was 101.6 and my entire body was slick with sweat. Two hours later, when my temperature hit 103, we headed back to the hospital. Fantastic. My freedom had been pretty short-lived. Like a prisoner who just got released from jail, then was arrested for jaywalking the second he tried to cross the street in front of the courthouse.

There were no commuters on the road at that time so we made the trip into the city in less than a half hour. At some point in the middle of the ride, a consultation took place between one of my parents and Dr. Balder. I don't remember which one and I don't remember what was said. I was a little blurry, to say the least. "Burning up" was more like it.

I don't remember much of what happened after I got to the hospital, either. They could have thrown me a "welcome back" party, for all I knew. But I'm pretty sure that wasn't the case. What I *am* sure of was that the staff ran every test imaginable on me, because that's what they always did.

My fever dropped toward morning, as fevers tend to do, and I woke up fairly clear-headed. Still, I didn't have the energy of a paralyzed slug. A clicking pump to my left forced liquid antibiotics through a clear plastic line into my left arm. *Not* the best fashion accessory I've ever seen.

"Maddie," my mom said when I opened my eyes, "you have an infection."

Gee, thanks for sharing.

"In my brain?" I asked. "I have an infection in my brain?"

Mom blinked, then swiped at her eyes. That was all the answer I needed.

Great, now I was back to being one step from the grave again. But at least I was past denial. *Waaaayy* past it. When Dr. Balder showed up an hour later, he seemed truly disappointed to see me and I have to say that, as nice as he is, the feeling was mutual.

I just let him talk. I was so weak that I was beyond asking questions. Plus, he didn't have much to say. I was still in the "evaluating" stage.

After Dr. Balder left, the testing-medication portion of the program started all over again. At ten o'clock, I was taken down to the radiology lab and given another MRI. But I was a veteran by then. The tunnel didn't bother me. The clanging didn't bother me. The results didn't bother me. Nothing bothered me. I was too numb and too exhausted to be bothered much by anything. My fate was out of my hands, and I knew it.

"We're going to monitor you closely," Dr. Balder explained when I got back to my room. "But if we don't see an improvement over the next twenty-four hours, we'll have to operate."

We? There's an old Paul Simon tune that my dad likes to listen to in his car. I don't remember the title, but the very first line is about how he'd rather be a hammer than a nail. Well, listening to Dr. Balder ramble on, I knew I'd rather be a surgeon than a patient. And there was no *we* to it. No matter what happened to Maddie Bergamo, when Dr. Balder's work was done, he'd go home to his family.

It was the same way with Coach Stover. Regardless of all her talk about teamwork and no matter how red she'd get, the players were the ones out on the court, busting our humps. She was safe on the sidelines.

But there was no point in arguing plural versus single subject. This wasn't English class, after all. Besides, I knew Dr. Balder was pulling for me. I just didn't know there was anything left to operate on.

I fell asleep a few minutes after Dr. Balder's visit. As I drifted off, I felt a twinge of guilt. Mom and Daddy looked like they were about an inch away from a meltdown. My job was to give them support, and here I was, putting them through all this again. Talk about strange. I was the patient, right? But I couldn't escape the feeling that I was somehow supposed to make it better for them. Maybe, if I were a little more coherent, I would have been angry. Instead, I felt only a sense of regret, as though I'd let the entire team down.

When I woke up later that afternoon, I sat up and saw that my parents were out of the room and there was a boy, maybe fifteen or sixteen, standing in the doorway. I didn't have to ask what he was doing at the Samuelson Hospital for Pediatric Neurology. He was so thin he could have been the poster boy for an eating disorder. His scalp was inflamed on one side and what little hair he had on his head stood out in tufts. The black circles around his eyes were big enough and dark enough to make a raccoon jealous.

"Hi, I'm Josh Grappinelli." He smiled and stepped into the room, totally and admirably unself-conscious. "From Bensonhurst. That's in Brooklyn."

My first thought was, *puh-leeeze*, Josh from Brooklyn? Come to cheer me up. I don't need cheering. I need surgery. But if my mind was dismissive, the rest of me wasn't listening to it. I felt a wave of gratitude sweep over me. My parents and the doctors and the nurses were all looking out for my body, my machine, but they couldn't know what I was going through, not really. That wasn't true for Josh. He'd been through everything I had, and more. That was obvious at a glance.

"I'm Maddie Bergamo, from Montclair. That's in New Jersey," I heard myself say a little snottily.

He put his bony hands in front of his face, like a boxer protecting himself from a blow. "Oh, a tough guy, huh? I better watch my step."

We both laughed. Then he said, "So, what bank did you rob?"

"Bank?"

"What are you in for?"

I dropped back on the pillow, suddenly tired again. But not so tired that I didn't spill my story. My *entire* life story. As if he'd asked.

I talked about basketball: how good I was and how many points I'd scored and, oh, yeah, how my leg suddenly stopped working during that one game. Then I told him about how I'd gone to the nurse's office and all about the Bengali Rose coming in to comfort me. I probably even mentioned how ugly her scarf was.

Josh listened patiently to the part about the initial tests and how I hoped it was just an inflammation (I liked using that word, now that I knew what it meant), and then the whole brain tumor thing. I threw in a "watch and wait" for old time's sake then went through the operation, the infection, and how I ended up back here.

He just nodded the whole time, never cutting in once with anything about himself. Selfish, that's what I was. As though I were the only person in the world who'd ever been through this ordeal. Though, clearly, that wasn't the case.

Luckily for Josh, toward the end of my story, my parents came back into the room and saved him from hearing the rest. They smiled in that way adults do when they're embarrassed and stopped about ten feet from the bed. I was glad they arrived when they did. Now I wouldn't have to explain the whole interracial thing. Can you spell boring?

"Hello," Dad said, "we're Maddie's parents."

"Hi, I'm Josh Grappinelli."

"From Bensonhurst," I added. "That's in Brooklyn."

Dad started to come forward, but Mom grabbed his arm, holding him back. Talk about a mind-your-own-business situation. Mom said, "We haven't had anything to eat all day. It's past time for a cafeteria run."

What did she think—we were on a date?

"Nice meeting you, Josh," my parents said.

"Same here." Josh waited until they were gone, then turned back to me. "Funny how sometimes you worry more about your folks than you do about yourself. You feel sorry for them because they're so scared. Know what I mean?"

"Yeah, totally. I know *exactly* what you mean." Boy, was I glad it wasn't just me. "So, what are you in for?"

"A radiation treatment."

"An astrocytoma?" I think I was trying to show off. As-tro-cy-to-ma. Dr. Maddie calling. But the way Josh shook his head brought me to a dead stop.

"A medulloblastoma." I have to admit, that was a new one on me. He compressed his lips for a moment then said, in a very clear voice, "It's malignant." He took a step closer. "I've already had surgery. My doctor told me I was lucky.

The surgery results in permanent deficits twenty percent of the time." He shrugged. "Who knows? Maybe I'll get lucky again. The survival rate after five years is fifty percent."

His matter-of-fact attitude struck me as almost too rational. Okay, I wasn't in denial anymore. But I certainly hadn't moved on to full acceptance of the situation. "Lucky? More like terminally unfair. How old are you?"

"I'll be sixteen in September."

For a minute or so, neither one of us spoke. I'm pretty sure we were both thinking the same thing: We're too young to be having this conversation, but that's the way it is. Finally, I said, "I feel like my whole life has been turned upside down."

"And you just want it to go back to the way it was," he said, completing my thought.

"Yeah, exactly. How'd you know?"

"Been there, done that. But you want to hear something funny?" He was looking directly into my eyes.

"Anything."

"Going back to the way it was? That's the only thing you *can't* have, no matter what happens. Something like this, it changes you, whether you get better or not."

I didn't get better, not that afternoon or that night.

After Josh had left—and we promised to see each other again soon—my fever returned. In the evening, it rose to 101 then leveled off. Dr. Balder came in around seven o'clock. He told us that my white blood cell count was elevated and that the antibiotic running into my veins was proving ineffective. Then, just to be consistent, he delivered some more bad news. The MRI that had been taken that morning revealed a fluid build-up—an edema—at the tumor site.

"The fluid can put the same kind of pressure on the brain as the tumor," he explained.

"Are we talking mass effect here?" I asked, showing off again.

"I think you should take this seriously, Maddie," he said firmly but kindly. "I'm going to schedule you for surgery tomorrow. If the antibiotics take hold overnight, we can always cancel. Otherwise, we'll have to clean out the infection and install a shunt to drain off the fluid as it accumulates."

Clean out the infection? I imagined dozens of tiny men armed with mops and buckets running around my brain. But I was too weak to argue. And this time, even Mom reined herself in. I mean, what was the point? There was no going back now. It was like Josh said: Something like this changes you. You learn to take things as they come. For me, who always wanted to find an immediate solution to whatever problem, it was a huge lesson to learn.

Dr. Balder left a few minutes later, and you can believe me when I tell you that the silence was deafening. Mom looked shattered by the news. Then she rallied, as I could always count on her to do.

She pulled her chair closer to the bed. "Baby, I brought Golden Lea's book with me. Would you like me to read another part to you?"

Funny, right? After getting a lecture from my dad about taking the book out of the house? But somehow I couldn't come up with a joke, and I just nodded my head. I guess my mom knew how much I needed it—and that Golden Lea would have wanted me to hear it.

Chapter 9

A LESSON IN LOVE

A IN'T EASY FOR a God-fearin woman to admit, but us slaves was mosly a superstitious bunch. Ignorance was the cause. Not Masta Harris, nor any other masta, wanted his slaves to knowed nothin cept how to do their jobs. I think I already splained bout the trouble I got myself into on accounta my learnin. Well, you takes any peoples and keep em ignorant, they gonna natrally fill in the missin parts with inventions of their own. The Wild Man of the Forest was one of em.

I don't rememba when I first heard bout the Wild Man. Seems like I knowed bout him all my life. Him and the Boogeyman and the Greasy Scratch and them ghosts that rose up out the graves to plague the livin. The Wild Man wandered round by night when the moon was high. He was scared to come close to the big house lessen Masta would shoot em, but he was right ready to snatch up any child who strayed too far from their cabin. Yes, sir, the Wild Man would take that child back to his cave and cook him in a pot of greens. And disobedient chirrens was his favorite kind.

My age at that time, bout fourteen, might seem a tad far removed from bein a child. I knowed I felt myself more close to bein a young woman than a girl. But when I heard that hammer draw back and turned round to sight Jack Trembley, I mighta been two years old again. I was scared to the point that I couldn't rightly move a muscle.

The white man standin fore me was so tall that Pa barely came up to his shoulders. And he was dressed in the skins of animals, even to the hat on his head. His hair was white and it flowed all out from under his hat like the tails of a cloud, and his beard was jus as white and jus as long. Underneath the brim of his hat, his green eyes shined like emeralds. It was the Wild Man himself, all right.

I spected to be snatched up straightaway, but the man jus busted out laughin. I looked at my pa and seen that Pa weren't scared, not thataway.

"Little girl, you are lookin at me like I have the intention of dinin on your bones." Jack Trembley had a formal way of talkin, but he didn't take his finger off the trigger of that long rifle he carried. "Well, let me assure you that while I have freely dined on much of what the Lord provides, I have not yet stooped to eatin chirrens."

"What you gonna do with us?" Pa asked. He was mad as a hornet, but there weren't nothin he could do bout that rifle. Jack Trembley didn't git them skins he wore by missin what he was shootin at.

"State your name," he said.

"Elijah. And this here is my daughter, Golden Lea."

"Well, Elijah, it seems you have come a long way from home."

"We ain't got no home," Pa said.

Jack Trembley laughed again. "No, I don't suppose a slave does have a home. Not to my way of thinkin. But that don't answer my question. Where have you come from? And where in the world do y'all think you headed?"

"We goin north," I said. "To Ohio."

"He knows where we goin," Pa said.

"Maybe he does, Pa, but it ain't polite not to answer a question." I looked up at Jack Trembley. "We come from Belle Maison, over in Clark County."

Pa looked at me like I was crazy, but he didn't say nothin. Then Jack Trembley pointed that long rifle away from us.

"My name is Jack Trembley," he said, "and I have lived free all my life. I have broken trail as far away as California and been down to Mississippi and lived for a time with the Comanche in Texas. Bondage don't appeal to me, though I have witnessed bondage in many forms, and I don't believe it appeals to the good Lord, neither. Mens was born to be free. Little girls, too."

"Well, then, we jus be on our way," Pa said.

"On your way to where? North? To Ohio? Elijah, you are not a man of the forest. You have been bruised by the limbs of trees and cut by thorns and briars. And you have traveled more easterly than north. At this rate, y'all as likely to find yourself in Virginia as Ohio. In case you don't knows it, Virginia is a slave state."

"Don't see how that matters," Pa said. "Cause there ain't no goin back."

"Be that as it may, Cloud Dreamer would have my hide if I didn't invite you to the cabin. Cloud Dreamer is my wife. It was she who taught me the ways of the Lord. I was pretty much lost till then."

119

Jack Trembley turned round and took a few steps. Then he turned back to us. "Come along now, we'll git you a hot meal," he said. "And there's a way north from here. I'll describe it to you over breakfast."

Neither me nor Pa moved a single inch. But we didn't walk off the other way, neither. Course, I can't speak for Pa, but a hot meal and a place to rest seemed mighty fine at that moment. Only trustin white folks was not somethin I was accustomed to. No, sir. The white folks I knowed up till then didn't think no more of me than they did of their pigs and cattle. And the ones that was mos close was the meanest.

Jack Trembley pointed to Pa's bag. "How much food you got left? Enough to last for a week?" He and Pa looked each other in the eye for a minute. Then Jack said, "Not even that much? Well, suit yourself, Elijah. If you feel you can make it on your own, go ahead. But you'd bes think bout that girl of yours. Don't matter whether you find your way north or continue east, cause you will soon run into the foothills of the Allegheny Mountains. By my word, that there is some rugged country."

Jack Trembley turned and started off again. Me and Pa, we looked at each other for a moment. We knowed Masta Harris would pay a reward to anyone who returned us to Belle Maison. And we knowed that Jack Trembley knowed it, too. But we also knowed that the man was right. We'd been travelin for two nights and we hadn't come but a little way. Our food would run out shortly.

Without sayin nothin, me and Pa started after Jack. We had to half-run to keep up, but it was a lot easier than crashin through the forest. Jack led us along game trails made by the animals livin in the woods. Those trails ran every whichaway, cuttin between the trees and round the rocks. To this day, I don't knowed how Jack found his way home.

But home is where we ended up, a two-room log cabin. The cabin was set in a small clearin with a wooden fence runnin all the way round. There was a little road out front, half-overgrown, and a vegetable patch in the back. A woman stood in the garden as we come into the clearin. She was wearin a deerskin dress that dropped down to her knees, and a string of blue and yella beads round her neck. Her skin was very red and she had plaited her hair into thick braids. She stared at me and Pa for a moment, then looked at the sky. The sun was up now.

"Bes git em inside," she said.

Our breakfast was nothin more than corncakes fried up with a little bacon and hot coffee. But it tasted mighty fine after them cold meals we been eatin. And it felt good to eat inside the cabin, too. Lookin back, I gotta say the cabin weren't much better than the cabins Masta Harris built for his slaves. There was only two small rooms and the scant furniture was rough-hewn. Seems like Jack Trembley was no kind of carpenter. Nor a mason, neither, judgin from the crooked fireplace he used for a stove. But it seemed right homey on that mornin.

I learned over my breakfast that Jack Trembley was a man who liked to hear himself talk. Cloud Dreamer was his exact opposite. She watched us close, but didn't speak more than a word or two. That's probly cause we was a danger to em, as we was a danger to any white man or woman who helped us escape. Course, at the time, I didn't knowed nothin bout white folks comin to the aid of escapin slaves. But it turned out there was white folks who didn't hold with slavery, even down South. Lands, but they had a mighty hard time if they was caught. The slave owners would jus as soon hang em as look at em. And what law there was in Kentucky was solid on the side of the big planters. Little folks like Jack Trembley and Cloud Dreamer didn't have no rights a'tall.

But if Cloud Dreamer didn't say much, when Jack tole the story of her peoples, it quickly come clear why she didn't have no love for white folks. Cloud Dreamer was born into the Cherokee nation way down south in Georgia. Now them Cherokees, they wasn't goin bout killin white folks. No, sir, they was civilized. They had their own schools and banks and churches. But none of that helped em one bit. Them white folks in Georgia passed a law said Cherokee land was now white folks' land and the Cherokees had to git out.

Natrally, the Cherokees resisted. Little good it did em. They was rounded up and marched all the way to Oklahoma—mens, womens, and chirrens, too. To hear Jack tell it, thousands died along the way, includin Cloud Dreamer's mama and her baby brother.

Cloud Dreamer didn't say one word all the while Jack was tellin the story. She was busy washin greens and cuttin root vegetables to make a soup. After she set the pot to boilin, she got up and went back out to the field behind the cabin.

"Don't mind Cloud Dreamer," Jack tole us. "She's a might upset cause I haven't brought back meat for the table. Last night, she tole me to fish, but I had a hankerin for fresh venison. Now, if I had been successful, she'd be all smiles. But she is not a woman to tolerate failure."

Pa hadn't said much till that point. As I mentioned fore, he weren't a big talker. But now he spoke up.

"Mista Trembley, you been right kind to us and I thanks you for me and my daughter both. But we got ourselfs a long way to go, so it's bes we be movin on."

Jack scratched at his beard for a minute, then said, "Well, if you want to resume your journey, I am not the man to stop you. But I believe it would be for the bes if you slep here till sunset. Now, I will not guide you to Ohio. The risk is too great. Cloud Dreamer and I are jus hangin on here as it is. But I can guide you to a creek that you can foller north into the mountains for a good twenty miles. That will put you within thirty miles of the Ohio River."

Pa looked at me and I could see in his eyes that he was torn in two. Mos likely, he was thinkin the safest place for us was in them woods. But we was awful tired after two nights trudgin through the forest. The sun was well up, too, and travelin by day was risky.

"Why you wanna help us?" Pa asked.

Jack Trembley jus shook his head. "When my peoples came to Kentucky from Pennsylvania, back bout the time of the Revolution, this here was all wilderness. A man, Indian or white, lived by his wits and his strength. We trapped and hunted and farmed some, and traded with the Choctaw when they came through in the summer. Tobacco changed all that. Tobacco and the slave owners who planted it. They took the bes land for themselfs. And it didn't matter how long a man had been livin on that land or what claim he filed with the county. The only law back then was the planters' law. They ran the county government and hired the county sheriff. The little farmers got pushed out to the margins, while men like myself, the hunters, were left with what nobody else wanted. So, I have no love for slave holders."

"That don't answer the question," Pa said. "It's one thing to hate the planters and another to help the likes of us."

Jack thought bout this, noddin when he come to some kind of conclusion. "Lord knows, in my life I have done some

123

awful things. I was a drinkin man fore Cloud Dreamer showed me the way. That is a sad excuse, I knows, but it is the only explanation I have to offer for the deeds I committed. Now I see that I must do more than pray. I see that I must atone and the only way I knowed is by practicin simple charity."

I don't believe that Pa was convinced. We was too long livin among slavers not to be suspicious, no matter how fine the man's words were. But we finally give in cause we was jus too tired to go on. That back room weren't much. There weren't no beds, jus two corn-shuck mattresses on the floor. There weren't no windows, neither, so it was already hot. But I fell asleep soon as I laid my head down.

"Golden Lea, wake up!"

I jerked awake right quick, not really knowin where I was. Then I heard hoof beats. There was horses comin, a number of em. I looked round the room, my heart knockin hard on my ribs. There weren't no way out, no windows or chimney or nothin. We was trapped.

"Pray, girl," Pa said. "Cause if ever we needed the Lord's help, it's now."

I didn't pray right then. I crawled over to the door, intendin to shut it. Jus fore I did, I seen Jack Trembley pick up that long rifle and go on out the front. He left the door open behind him and me and Pa, we could hear right good. First thing, the horses come to a stop, snortin and stampin like they been runnin a long time. Then we heard Jack's voice and he seemed right irritated.

"I believe I have tole you more than once, Mista Markham, not to gallop up to my door. If you can't approach as a gentleman, stay away."

"Now, don't you git yourself all in a lather, Trembley. We're your friends and neighbors."

"Friends? Markham, I feel it would be in your interest not to insult me again. State your business and be gone."

"We're lookin for a pair of runaway slaves. A man name of Elijah and a girl name of Golden Lea. They escaped from Harris Jackson's place, Belle Maison."

Jack Trembley laughed. "Me and Jackson, we never did git along. I once challenged him to a duel. Do you knowed what he said? He said a man of his class would not soil himself by engagin with a man of mine."

"Be that as it may, we're ridin all through these hills, lettin everybody know."

"What makes you think these escaped slaves come this way? Jackson's place is a fair piece to the west."

"No special reason. We're jus soundin the alert. Alvin Kraft's got his bloodhounds out and I spect he'll come up behind em. Anyway, if you find em, they're worth one hundred dollars each. That's alive. But Harris Jackson's so mad, I spect he might even pay for em dead."

One hundred dollars each? I added the numbers in my head. Two hundred dollars. Jack Trembley didn't have much in this world. He and Cloud Dreamer was wearin skins stead of reglar clothes and his raggedy cabin would near mos fit on the porch at Belle Maison. Nor did they own so much as a cow or a pig, and even the horse they had in a little corral was old and swaybacked.

"Dead?" Jack Trembley said. "That's not like Harris Jackson. No, the man I knew was as greedy as an infant. Those slaves won't be worth nothin dead."

"Harris is mighty furious, Jack. He claims he had an offer for the slave name of Elijah. Fifteen hundred dollars. But now that Elijah's run away, the deal is off."

"I'm sorry to have to say so, but that don't seem to me a reason for killin him." Jack Trembley stopped right there, but Markham didn't say nothin and Jack finally spoke again. "Mista Markham, I knowed you to be a churchgoin man. Do you believe the Lord will look upon this moment with favor when it comes your turn to stand before Him?"

"Well, I don't rightly knows, Jack. Myself, I don't figure the Lord weighs killin a slave equal to killin a white man. Iffen He did, He wouldn't have made em slaves in the first place."

That said, Markham and his patrollers rode out the way they come. Me and Pa listened to the hoof beats till they was too faint to hear. Then I busted out cryin.

I was so tired of bein scared.

We had ourselfs some dinner, a vegetable soup laced with dried venison and a flat kinda bread Cloud Dreamer made directly on the rocks in the fireplace. The sun had set by the time we was finished. Cloud Dreamer took Pa's bag and filled it with some of that dried venison and flatbread. She didn't talk much as she went bout her work. Jus hummed to herself. I figured she didn't like havin us round, but after dinner, she and Jack went outside and had themselfs a conversation. A few minutes later, they come back in, and Cloud Dreamer went direct to a big wooden trunk and opened it. She stuck her arm in that trunk and fiddled round till she come up with a small brass case. She brought this to us and put it in Pa's hand. Natrally, it was Jack Trembley who spoke. "Open that up, Elijah." He waited till Pa unlatched the round cover and pulled it back. *There was a glass inside and a little arrow beneath that floated back to point in the same direction when Pa turned the case from side to side. "Do you knows what that is, Elijah?"*

"I knows," I said. "Masta Harris had one jus like it. That there is a called a compass." I pointed to the tip of the arrow. "And that there's north."

Jus sayin the word brought me courage. North. That probly don't sound like much to folks today. But the word was magic for slaves. North meant freedom. North was the Promised Land.

"I was given that compass as a reward for leadin a party of land surveyors into the Dakota Territory," Jack Trembley said. "That was back in '33 and the Sioux were on the warpath. I've kep it all these years, but Cloud Dreamer tells me I have to give it over. Well, I have no need of the instrument anyhow. The day I can't tell north from south is the day I hope to be stretched out in my pine box."

Pa looked down at the brass compass, then at me, then at Jack Trembley. "I don't rightly knowed what to say."

"Then hold your peace, Elijah, and let's be off."

Good advice, I must admit. But I did hesitate long enough to do one more thing. I run up to Cloud Dreamer and give her a hug. She hugged me right back and whispered in my ear.

"Trust," she tole me. "Trust in the Lord with your whole heart and soul and He will lift you up no matter how terrible the moment."

I can't say I was happy bout leavin Jack and Cloud Dreamer's little cabin. The night was cool and them woods was very dark as Jack led us along those game trails. I knowed what he was bout. There weren't no horse could come the way we come. But I swear I was lost fore we covered a mile. And Jack, he didn't slow down for a minute, jus led us forward till we come to a creek an hour later. The creek was near wide enough to float Jack's cabin, but it was late summer and the water was down. Still, followin the creek wouldn't be no easy task. There was rocks all along the bottom and the water was runnin hard down the center.

"Well, folks, I've brought you as far as I'm able, given the circumstances. This creek winds some, especially in them mountains, but it will bring you far to the north fore it peters out. Watch for farms as you go along. There are a number on the creek and you'll have to skirt em."

"What bout the Ohio River?" Pa asked. "Can it be swum?"

"No, Elijah, it can't. The river is too wide and the currents too swift. You'll need a boat. Now I've heard tell there are mens along that border who are willin to row a slave across the Ohio. Mens who don't hold with human bondage. But there are others who will turn you in for the reward. How you separate one from the other is beyond my explanation."

When Jack Trembley stopped speakin, the night closed round us. We listened to the water runnin hard over them rocks and the wind cryin in them trees. Up ahead, an owl hooted, once, then again. Finally, Pa spoke up.

"Me and Golden Lea, we don't knows how to thank you, Mista Trembley. But I believes the Lord will surely bless you for what you done."

"Well, I'm sure glad to hear that, Elijah. Cause I'm a man in need of all the blessings I can git."

Without another word, he turned on his heel and headed off, movin so swift through the trees he mighta been half-animal *himself. And we was left alone, me and Pa, with the moonlight on the water and the stars in the sky.*

As we begin trudgin through the rocks and briars along the creek, my hopes was high. Jack Trembley and Cloud Dreamer were proof positive that there's another world out there. That it ain't all Belle Maison and the rule of the whip.

Chapter 10

THE SOUND OF SILENCE

I WOKE UP in the hospital's intensive care unit the next morning. My fever hadn't fallen, as fevers usually do toward sunrise, and I was barely able to speak. But I could hear Dr. Balder well enough when he came into the room at eight o'clock. The words he used—infection, surgery—didn't bother me all that much. I'd heard them before. The grave tones, however, were new to me.

Dr. Balder's words were hopeful. He would reopen my skull and "clean out" the infection. The surgery would be faster and simpler than the earlier "procedure." So why, then, did he sound as if he were going to a funeral? I guess not all doctors were good actors, after all.

I don't know. I was pretty much out of it that morning. Major. My body felt like it was pinned to the bed and the fever wasn't helping, either. Maybe I was making it up as I went along. Maybe I only imagined the hopelessness in his voice. But it seemed to me that my parents were having an omigosh-we're-losing-our-only-daughter moment. You know, sucking it up, staying brave for the sake of the child? Daddy looked down and shook his head, like he couldn't believe this was happening. Me neither, Dad.

"Maddie?" Dr. Balder's voice seemed to come from a great distance. I tried to answer him, but my mouth didn't want to form the words.

Finally, I said, "Yes?" It wasn't exactly earth-shattering, but it took all the strength I had.

"If you want, we can give you something to relax you before the surgery."

Relax? Oh, yeah, that'd be great. If I were any more relaxed, I'd be a throw pillow. I shook my head and closed my eyes, and my sense of time simply vanished. I couldn't tell you if I waited one hour or ten before I was taken down to the operating suite. Throughout, my parents stood on either side of the bed, holding onto my hands. Trying not to cry.

What's that business about there being no atheists in foxholes? At Christmas and Easter, like clockwork, and from time to time the rest of year, the Bergamo family attended Sunday Mass at Redeemer Church, one of Montclair's many Catholic churches. I'd made my First Communion at Redeemer, though it seemed like a hundred years before I got sick. So, I'd have to say that although I believed in God, I wasn't really all that religious. Now I felt myself reaching back for something.

My first thought was that my life hadn't been worth very much. I was neither a saint, nor a sinner. Like any other kid, my thoughts were tuned to the future and my wonderful plans. Plans for what, though? To be a basketball star? To get asked to the dance by some boy I didn't even know because my friends and I thought he was cute? To spend a summer in Europe before I graduated high school? To wear the prettiest clothes, and listen to the hippest music, and have the coolest friends, and go to the best college?

I was beginning to realize that every minute of life is precious, that without warning, anyone can be laid low. I was beginning to realize that humility isn't some kind of act; it's not something to be put on, like a dress from a new designer. Humility is what happens to you when you open your eyes and admit how small you really are.

Just before they came for me, I made a promise. I don't know who I made the promise to. God, I guess, but I didn't say the word. Only that if I came through this with my brain in one piece, I'd stop being selfish. I promised not to live a trivial life and that I'd put substance ahead of style. Yes, I was born into the bling-bling generation. Yes, my dreams were designer dreams. But I would find a better way.

I remembered what Josh Grappinelli from Bensonhurst, Brooklyn, said. With something this big, there's no going back to what you were. If you try, you're doomed to eternal disappointment. You can only embrace what you've become—assuming you live long enough to discover what that is—and then work harder at making changes that are bigger than yourself.

Anyway, that's what I promised right before they came to wheel me into surgery.

I woke up after my surgery to find myself lost in a nightmare. I was back in the intensive care unit and Mom was leaning down over the bed. I could see her lips moving and hear the sounds she made, but I couldn't understand a word. I couldn't speak, either. Words came into my mind, and then whole sentences, but when I tried to say them out loud, nothing happened. Believe me, it made not being able to read seem like a walk in the park. On a beautiful day. In Paris.

The most bizarre part was that my brain was working just fine and I could still think. Which wasn't all that much of a break. I mean, all I could think about was being trapped inside my own mind forever. "Permanent neurological deficits" was a phrase that Dr. Balder and Josh Grappinelli had both used. And it was the one I couldn't get out of my mind just then. The only thing accompanying that frightening thought was the sound of my mother's incoherent words and the rapid beating of my own heart.

That wasn't the only thing. Did I forget to mention the pain? My head hurt so much that I thought it might split apart. Instinctively, I raised my hand to the side of my head, only to discover a tube running through a bandage taped to my scalp. I traced the tube to a small plastic bulb pinned to the bed sheet and was somehow reassured. Okay, there was a beginning and an end, and probably a purpose for it. Then I discovered a second tube running into my nose and down my throat. I didn't have a clue about what that tube was supposed to accomplish or where it ultimately ended, though I could take a few gross guesses.

A dozen questions flashed through my mind, but I was unable to speak a single word. Probably the word I would have spoken at that moment was "terrifying."

Daddy had joined Mom and they both looked as if they'd crossed a line somewhere. Now Mom was crying and it was my father's turn to try to offer comfort. Behind the bed, a heart monitor kept a steady beat: boop, boop, boop, boop. Regular as the metronome on my music teacher's piano. That was definitely a good sign. Score one for positive thinking.

Trapped as they were, my thoughts at the time were not just of my mom and dad, but of Golden Lea and her father, Elijah, deep in the Kentucky woods. I envisioned them from above, a bird's-eye view of two very small people alone and lost in a wilderness that stretched away in all directions. I wondered if I'd ever hear the end of her story, or if they'd stay like that, frozen in time within my mind forever. They deserved a better ending than that. Not to be stuck in limbo, like me.

I was so weary I could barely move, and I felt myself growing even weaker. For the first time in my life, I saw death as a destination I would inevitably reach. The funny part is that I wasn't afraid. Death seemed almost peaceful, a release from the pain and all the craziness. For sure, it was a lot better than being trapped inside my mind, completely isolated and nobody knowing what I was thinking or even that I was still capable of thought. For a few horrifying seconds, I wondered if this is what being in a coma was like until someone mercifully pulled the plug.

Thankfully, that train of thought was cut short when a nurse came into the room and gave me something else to focus on: the needle in her hand. She injected me with some kind of pain medication and I drifted off to a place without time or definition. I was nowhere. I was everywhere. Then I finally sunk into a dream.

I was in the Eagle Rock Reservation on the outskirts of Montclair, walking along a trail that circled First Mountain.

Mountains are supposed to be majestic, I know, but First Mountain was more of a hill, rising only about six hundred feet above sea level. Its real claim to fame was the view from the summit over the flat lands to the east. Manhattan was fifteen miles away and the New York City skyline was visible on any clear day. A glimpse of the urban jungle from the suburban wilderness.

In the dream, I was far from the summit. Eagle Rock includes more than four hundred acres of wandering trails that lead across hills and valleys. The reservation is also heavily forested and some of the trails cover miles of ground without ever reaching the summit. I didn't know which trail I was on, or whether it would lead to the top. The forest was thick on both sides and the branches of the trees arched overhead to crisscross in the middle, so that I felt I was walking through a tunnel. The only sound was the crunching of my feet on the dried leaves underfoot and I saw none of the usual forest animals: neither birds, nor squirrels, nor rabbits. I was utterly lost and alone.

I made steady progress, though, leaping easily across the occasional stream. I felt no anxiety whatsoever, and my step was light. Curiosity was driving my little ramble. What was around the next bend? Over the next hill? Something good, I was sure, something fabulous. Better, even, than the breathtaking view of the city.

I'd hiked these trails before, with Mom or Dad, or sometimes both. Always, they'd been crowded with hikers, but now I was in complete solitude, which is maybe how it's supposed to be. Four hundred acres may sound like a lot, but there were hundreds of thousands of people living only a short distance away. The reservation was more like an oasis than the forested wilderness Elijah and Golden Lea hiked through. Still, something about my journey echoed theirs. I was trying to find my way somewhere. To a new home? To freedom?

My sense of time wasn't too sharp, but it seemed as if I had walked for hours. Yet the light remained constant, as if the sun had stopped moving, and it was soft and caressing, a pleasure that grew more intense the further I went. Some part of me kept expecting night to fall. Another part knew that it never would.

Though I didn't give it a moment's consideration at the time, I was in perfect health. My hair was elaborately braided, the braids shot through with a rainbow of beads, and I wore a loose-fitting dress, almost a robe, that reached my calves. I might have been a bride led to a wedding, except that there was no one to lead me and I knew I wouldn't find a husband on the other end. I didn't have a clear understanding, but a fuzzy remembrance of lights and tunnels and what they signified was lurking somewhere in the back of my mind—in the portion that wasn't dreaming. I'd heard that people who had near-death experiences came back and talked of these things. And the ones who didn't come back? Well, I guess they reached the light.

I came to an end of sorts, finally, when I reached the summit and walked onto a plaza dedicated to the men and women who died in the attack on the World Trade Centers on September 11, 2001. The light here was dazzling. It shimmered in the near and far distance, dancing around the blocky outlines of Manhattan's office towers, as it danced around the memorial's simple sculptures: first and foremost, a massive bronze book that displayed the names of the Essex County residents killed in the 9/11 attack. Then a narrow, rough-hewn pillar that rose from behind the book to support an enormous bronze eagle in flight. A little girl, also bronze, stood before the book, facing outward. She wore a long dress and cradled a teddy bear against her chest.

I doubt if there was a resident of Montclair, or of any of the surrounding towns, who hadn't been to the memorial. School kids, including me, were taken to the memorial on class trips. But I barely looked at the statues, or at the granite walls to either side, inscribed with the names of all those who died on 9/11.

My attention was taken up by a diminutive black woman, old and stooped and very dark. She was wearing a white apron over a gingham dress. She was facing away from me, looking out across the valley toward Manhattan and the slanting rays of sun that gilded the skyscrapers. Even though I couldn't see her face—and I'd never seen her before anyway—I did know who she was.

"I went all the way to Chicago once," the woman said without turning around. "That was in the year 1876. My, but Chicago was somethin' to behold. All that hustle and bustle. As the Lord is my witness, some of them buildings musta been fifty feet high."

She paused, and though I couldn't see her expression, I knew she was smiling. "But even in my dreams, I never thought to see nothin' like this." She gestured toward the New York City skyline. "Seems like progress has gone plumb crazy."

Finally, she turned to face me, and I was immediately drawn to her eyes. They were bright, almost feverish, and clearly filmed by cataracts. I might have asked myself, at that time, how she could possibly see Manhattan, but I never thought to doubt her, not for a minute.

"Girl," she said, "you gotta go back the way you come. You got work to do."

"What kind of work?" I asked, in awe.

"The work of your life."

I walked by her and around the sculptures. Now my view of the city was unobstructed.

"It's not fair." My voice was utterly calm. I might have been reading the items on a shopping list. "I'm only fourteen. I'm not supposed to have a brain tumor, or get an infection, or suffer permanent neurological deficits. I'm just a kid."

The woman walked over to join me. Her steps were slow and hesitant, the soles of her high-button shoes scraping the pavement. "My daughter tells me I should use a cane. She claims my walkin' on my own is due to my vanity. Vanity? Well, I do believe my husband thought me a rare beauty once, but he was 'bout the only one." She laughed to herself with the memory of it.

I felt her come up behind me and put her hand on my shoulder. Her fingers were all bones. It was as if we'd known each other all our lives, and I wasn't particularly surprised to see her.

"Isn't it beautiful?" I said. "New York. Every kid in my class wants to live in New York City someday."

Golden Lea Jackson laughed, a gleeful cackle. "Someday ain't today. And fair don't have nothin' to do with nothin'. If you should think it does, go read them names, the ones in the book and on the wall." She pointed to the inscribed granite wall and the bronze book. "What was they doin', 'cept goin' to work like they done every mornin'? And how much you think they'd give to have one more day with their families?" She paused. "Now you got the rest of your life to live—no matter how long or short it is—and you need to get on with it."

"Do you have the answer to that?" I asked, almost afraid to ask the question.

"About how long you're goin' to live?" She smiled. "Child, don' you worry none 'bout that. You're gonna live for the rest of your life."

I didn't move. I just stood there and let it all sink in. With all of her wisdom and all of her experience, she knew I still had some work to do, however long it took. Then I stopped thinking about myself.

I turned to her and asked, "What did you think when you were running away through the forest? Did you hate them all?"

"All of what?"

"White people. The slave owners."

"The skeeters and the rocks, them was what I hated," she sighed. "When you cross over rocky ground at night, seems like there's no place to lay your foot without scrapin' your ankle. And the skeeters? Only thing I can't figure is how they didn't suck out every drop of blood from my body."

"That's not really an answer."

"Madison Bergamo, what I got to say 'bout them times, I wrote in my recollections. If y'all want to know how it come out, you got to go back and read my words for your own self." She seemed to be smiling as she scolded me. A trait passed down to my mother. "But know this: There ain't no point in hate. How could I hate all white people on the earth for the actions of Masta and the other slave owners in the southern United States? And how could I hate Masta for being born in them times and havin' them notions that we now know is wrong? Why, that would be like you hatin' them cells in your body what were notioned wrong and turned bad. Best you could hope for is that the badness don't spread and somethin' happens to change them 'round. But hate ain't it. Hate jus' makes your whole self sick. It ain't no kind of cure."

I listened to her words, then looked again at the towers of Manhattan. They were still there, still shimmering with promise, and I felt light enough to simply fly across the miles on my own. All I had to do was leap into the air and ride the wind across the Hudson River. But Golden Lea's firm grip on my arm held me in place.

I looked at her, summoning up my courage. "Is there a secret?" I asked. "Something I need to know?"

She took a few seconds to consider. "Yes, there's somethin' you need to know. But it ain't no secret—the Lord gave it to us in the Good Book. Fact, let me say this: All love is love of the Lord. True love between a man and a woman. Love for a child. A farmer's love of the land. My pa's love for horses. Maddie, I tells you that peoples who live without ever lovin' nothin' are the worst off peoples there is. And there ain't no amount of money or trinkets or medical concoctions that can make them well." She paused, and I swear her whole face lit up with sunlight and glimmered more brilliantly than the buildings she was staring at. I remember thinking that the name "Golden" couldn't have suited her better.

141

Then she continued. "Most of all, rememba this, child: Love God with all your heart, and love other peoples the way you want to be loved. 'Specially them that is most lowly."

I turned my attention to the skyline once more and when I looked back toward Golden Lea, she was gone.

My fever continued through the night and the pain in my head was unceasing, despite the painkillers I was injected with. I was delirious for much of the time, and wished for delirium when I was lucid. I still couldn't talk or understand anything spoken to me. And my father didn't make it any better when he tried to communicate by writing messages on a notepad. The letters might have been characters etched on the walls of an Aztec temple for all they meant to me.

But if I couldn't read what Daddy wrote, I could feel his love for me, and Mom's, too. I tried to concentrate on Golden Lea's words: Their love was true love, and that was the kind of strength that could help anyone get through even the worst times.

The one overriding thing that this sickness taught me was that my future was far from certain; everybody's was. Even before I got sick, no matter how sewn up I thought my future was, it wasn't. All my plans were just plans. All my hopes were just hopes. Everything could change in an instant—and it did. Except, of course, true love. That was constant.

Even though I was still lost in the forest, like Golden Lea and her father, I wasn't afraid of where the path would lead or what my future would bring. The only way to go was forward.

The antibiotics finally kicked in the next morning, shortly after the sun rose to fill the room's large single window. I woke up without a fever, but still too weak to do more than lie there with my eyes fixed on the light in the window. It looked so much like the light in my dream.

My parents were off to my left, both asleep on the reclining armchairs. Finally, it occurred to me that maybe I'd fooled Golden Lea Jackson. I mean, I had no memory of returning back through the trail on the Eagle Rock Reservation, but I'd made it to New York City in spite of her. After all, the hospital was on Fifth Avenue.

Okay, so it wasn't much of a joke. But gimme a break, *puh-leeeze*? For the morning after surgery, it wasn't all that bad. It was enough to make me laugh, anyway. Out loud!

Mom's eyes opened and she came to her feet so fast I thought she was going to jump over the bed. Maybe she mistook my laugh for a death rattle.

"Baby, baby, baby," she said.

A good minute passed before I realized that I understood the words. Mom was staring down at me, her hair in tatters and her eyes streaked with red. I wanted to comfort her, but I still couldn't speak. Mom tried to smile, then said, "Talk to me, honey."

I laughed again, another good joke. Then Mom took my hand and I squeezed down hard enough to make an impression. There were things I wanted to say so badly.

My father's face appeared a moment later and the two of them began to speak. This time, I tuned out deliberately. I understood the words, but I had something else on my mind. I squeezed down on my mother's hand again, then again.

143

"Do you want something, baby?" Mom asked.

Well, yea-uh. Only I couldn't tell her what it was. We had to play a little game in which she asked question after question. It was like charades for sick people. Was I in pain? Did I need to use the bathroom? Was I thirsty? Hungry? Did I want to speak to the nurse? The doctor? I think they would have summoned the president if I asked. Which would have been great, except I wouldn't have been able to say anything.

But, to tell the truth, I had no interest in the president at the moment, or in the doctor or the nurse. And I was too weak to be hungry. I was fixated on my great-great-great-grandmother, Golden Lea Jackson, and her story.

Finally, Mom got the hint. She must have seen it in my eyes. When she asked if I wanted to hear the next part of Golden Lea's *Recollections*, I squeezed down on her hand with all the strength I had left in my body.

Chapter 11

A HELPING HAND

W E TRUDGED THROUGH *what remained of that dark night, and then me and Pa made camp in a birch thicket high upon a hill, away from the creek. I rememba givin thanks to the Lord as I watched the risin sun edge the clouds on the horizon with purest gold.*

Sometimes, when I look back, I reckon I musta been the dumbest critter ever born upon the good Earth. After Jack Trembley gave Pa that compass and guided us to that creek, I figured my troubles was over. As if that there creek was some kinda pathway leadin directly to the Promised Land. Well, I'm alive to say that walkin along a stream is a sight better than cuttin through a forest, but it sure ain't a stroll through Mistriss Sarah's flower garden, neither.

First thing, the creek bed, even where there weren't no water, was mosly rocks washed down from the hills. Walkin cross em woulda been hard enough in daylight when a body could see where she was puttin her feet. But the way it was, my feets slipped down between them rocks every step I took and we didn't come more than a mile fore I was bruised right up past my ankles. And where there weren't no rocks, there was sand and mud that sucked at my feet like it was tryin to swallow me up. Me and Pa, we tried walkin up on the banks of the creek, only the trees in mos places hung over the water. Walkin on the bank weren't no different from walkin through the forest.

Then we come upon that grizzly bear.

Nowadays, when I tell my grand-chirrens the story bout that big ol bear, I finds it right humorous. But it weren't no fun when it happened, not for no young girl who was raised in Belle Maison and didn't knowed nothin bout the ways of the forest.

The creek mosly run fast, as I said, but in places where the land was flat, the water piled up into a pool. Toward dawn the second night after we left Jack Trembley's cabin, we come round a bend to find one of these pools directly ahead. The bear was right in the middle of the pool, half in the water and half out. I don't knowed what he was doin—drinkin, fishin, or takin a bath. No, sir, what I saw was that he was big and his paws was the size of my head and his teeth was long as my fingers. Then he rose up on his hind legs and sniffed the air and commenced to roar.

Me and Pa froze like we was turned to stone. My heart near dropped down through my feet and I couldn't draw nary a breath. Then Pa grabbed me up and turned to run. At the same time, the bear skedaddled in the opposite direction. To this day, I don't knowed which one of us was more scared—me and Pa or that ol grizzly. What I do knowed is that I didn't let Pa git more than a foot away from me that day. And I don't reckon I slep more than a minute or two. I was spectin that ol bear to come back and eat me right up. And, let me tell you, I weren't afeared of that ol Wild Man of the Forest no more.

On the followin night, we happened on the brown and gray farm dog. This turned out to be much more serious than that big ol bear. We was on the banks of the creek, restin, when the animal come outta the woods. This time, there was no sniffin round. He come straight at us with his ears pulled back and the hair long his spine stickin straight up. Pa pushed me behind him and grabbed up a branch, but he was too late. That dog bit deep into Pa's leg fore Pa smacked him hard enough to make him let go. He weren't through, though. No sir, that ol dog come right back, barkin and growlin, and Pa had to smack him again fore he finally lit off.

Pa didn't waste no time. There was no tellin who the dog had roused. Not fifteen minutes fore, we had passed by a little farm and the dog mos likely come from there. We took off along the creek and kep on goin till we covered some miles and the dawn was breakin. Then Pa rolled up his pants to clean his wound in the water.

The bite was deep into Pa's calf and I seen right away that we was in trouble. The wound wasn't bleedin jus that minute, but it had bled plenty fore. Pa's trouser leg was soaked and there was blood all down his shoe. I tore a strip of the hem off the long skirt I was wearin and tried to wash it in the creek. I wasn't foolin no one, not me or my pa. After all them nights hikin, our clothes was caked with mud and dust. But they was all I had and I done my bes to get it clean.

Pa was hobbled up good by the time the sun come to set that evenin. He fashioned himself a walkin stick from the branch of a fallen hickory, but it was mighty slow goin. And it didn't git no better the next night when the creek slowed to a trickle, then disappeared. There was forest all round us now, and the wind was whistlin through the pines like the heavens themselfs was beggin for mercy. I opened Jack Trembley's round brass compass and matched the way the floatin needle was pointin with the North Star. The points didn't match exactly, but they was close enough. When there was clouds coverin the stars, or the trees was too thick to see the sky, that there compass would guide us.

All the other problems with makin our way through a forest was still with us. There was swampy places to go round and farms to skirt and we couldn't travel straight north. Jack Trembley, he was right, too. This was rough land we was crossin now. The hills we run into, they wasn't no more than a coupla hundred feet high, but they was mighty steep and there was a plenty of em, as if the good Lord took the Earth and folded it into pleats. I rememba that every time I come up to the top of one of them hills, I was hopin to see the Ohio River. But for a long time, all I saw was another hill.

Pa didn't git no better, either. His leg reddened up round the wound and developed pus which I cleaned out as bes I could. There were womens back at Belle Maison who knowed how to collect wild plants and make a hot poultice to draw the pus out. Bein Missy Ann's personal slave, I didn't have much contact with em. And even if I had, me and Pa was deathly afraid of makin a fire and there weren't no way to heat the water. There weren't nothin I could do.

So, we jus kep on, me prayin by night and day till my words all run together in my head. I tole the Lord that I knowed His ways was mysterious and that I also knowed I had to accept His wisdom. I said I knowed if I trusted Him, like Cloud Dreamer tole me, I would find my reward when my time come to stand before His throne. But I was still askin for Him to heal my pa *in the here and now. I couldn't help myself. I loved my pa too much to do anythin else.*

Toward mornin on the followin night, we run into a storm. The lightnin come fast and thick, and the wind was jus whippin through the branches of the trees. We was soaked in a short minute and the rain didn't stop fallin for near two hours. By the time the sun rose, Pa had himself a fever.

The fever only run for a short time that first mornin. Pa was cool by the time evenin come and we shared the little food we had left from Jack Trembley's cabin. That was another thing we was gonna have to face. The hope was that the next hill would bring us to Ohio, but the truth was we mighta had miles and miles to go. There weren't no way to measure the distance we come and we was runnin short of food.

There's times when problems go round and round in your mind like fightin cats. That's on accounta there ain't no good answers. As evenin come and we began to hike through the woods, I was steady thinkin that Pa's wound needed a doctor's touch. The swellin was up and his fever had come back hard and we wasn't gettin no place, neither. I was thinkin that if we give ourselfs up, Pa would git some treatment. Like any slave, he weren't worth nothin dead.

So, we made slow progress that night, jus like the night fore. The hills became steeper and more steeper, till it reached the point where comin down was near as hard as goin up. Dawn was still far off when we finally come on a small farm in a valley. Pa said he couldn't go no further. After searchin round for a bit, we laid up in a thicket of pine trees on a hill lookin out over the farm. We could have gon over to the far side of the hill where I was sure we wouldn't be seen. We was plumb outta food ceptin for a few small pieces of dried venison, but I knowed full well there was food on that farm.

I believe I have already said that plantations big as Belle Maison weren't right common in Kentucky. Fact, mos peoples who kep slaves was small farmers and they didn't own but one or two. That was definitely the case on this here farm I was watchin.

Round dawn, a black man come out the little barn— weren't really no more than a shed—haulin a skinny milk cow on a rope. He walked that cow up to a small pasture near wheres the forest started and let the animal loose to graze. When he come back to the house, he knocked on the door and a white woman come out with a plate of food. That woman weren't dressed much better than her slave.

The farm covered maybe a coupla acres, planted mosly in tobacco, but also includin vegetables and melons. A pen near the house held a big ol sow and a passel of piglets and there was chickens runnin free in the yard. There was a dog, too, and that worried me some till I seen the dog was old and weak on its legs. The animal laid itself in the shade of an apple tree and barely moved the whole day long.

I fell asleep then, for a few hours. When I woke up, the whole family, husband and wife and a boy bout twelve years old, was in the fields, along with their slave. Lands, they was workin hard. And there weren't no difference in the work they done, neither. These was some poor peoples. Without everyone toilin from dawn to dusk, they wouldn't have nothin a'tall.

Pa woke up late in the afternoon. His fever was cooled, but his leg was swollen near double round his ankle, and lines of black ran down from the center of the wound to his foot.

He lay there for a little while, lookin out at the work goin on in the field.

"Golden Lea, what you got in mind?" he finally asked.

There weren't no foolin my pa and I didn't try. "I'm thinkin that come dark, I'm gonna sneak onto that farm and git us some food. You gotta eat, Pa, to keep your strength up."

Pa reckoned on this for a time, then he said, "That slave, he's gonna come to the meadow to fetch the cow fore nightfall. You git yourself hid in them bushes and call to em when he comes out. See if he'll do his Christian duty. Sneakin all the way down to the house is jus too risky. That dog there, he don't look like much, but if he picks up your smell, he will surely make a ruckus."

Now, all this talk bout stealin food might seem strange, what with me claimin to be a servant of the Lord. But neither me nor Pa thought we was doin wrong. If things was different and there was no slavers and slaves, I woulda gon right up to the door and asked for help. That would be the proper thing to do. But it was the slavers themselfs who closed off that path. It was the slavers who made thievin the only possibility.

The woman left the field halfway through the afternoon. Her arms was filled with vegetables for the evenin meal. Coupla hours later, the others quit. They walked together back toward the house, but only the father and his son went inside. Their slave weren't no more welcome than that pig in its pen. A few minutes later, the woman opened the door and handed her slave a plate of food.

I made my way through the forest to the edge of the meadow and settled down to wait. I didn't have to wait long. The man ate his dinner quick, then left his plate at the door and come walkin toward the meadow. I was afraid that when I spoke to him, he'd jump clean out his skin and run screamin back to the house. But there weren't nothin I could do but try.

"Mista," I whispered, "please don't turn round."

The man didn't turn and he weren't scared, neither. "Saw you up on that hill, girl. You lucky it was me and not the masta. Masta don't truck with runaways." He looked at me out the corner of his eyes. "Lands, but if you ain't a mess. How long you been in these woods?"

I tried to reckon back the days, but I couldn't rightly rememba. Days was somethin didn't concern me. Miles was what counted.

"Five, six days, maybe more. We come from Clark County."

"Well, you sure come a long way. What's your name, little lady? Mine's Silas."

"Golden Lea," I said. "My pa's hid in the woods. He got bit by a dog and his leg's swole up bad. We ain't got nothin to eat, neither."

"And you wants me to help y'all? That right?"

"I knows I don't have no right to ask, but we is pretty near desperate."

Silas looked at me hard for a minute, then his eyes relaxed. "I had me a daughter, once, a daughter and a wife. After Masta died, they was sold off to Alabama. My girl be right bout your age now. Her name is Athena."

"That's why me and Pa run off," I tole him. "Masta Harris had an offer on Pa and was gonna sell him. I done already lost my mama thataway."

Silas didn't answer right then. He walked up to the milk cow and gave it a right smart slap on the haunches. The cow bellowed once, then started off for the barn, takin her time bout it. Silas watched the animal go, shakin his head. "That *cow is bout the dumbest animal in Kentucky. Every evenin I comes out to bring her to the barn and every evenin I has to slap her rump to git her movin. Anyway, you go on back to your daddy. Come full dark, I'll bring along whatever food I can git my hands on."*

Pa was real sick when I got to him. His fever was up again and he was talkin nonsense bout some horse named Buckwheat. I tried to tell him what happened with Silas, but he didn't understand nary a word. I spect I shoulda been worried bout Silas, but I didn't believe he'd betray us. That's on accounta he mighta done it when he seen us in the afternoon. But I admit, I had me a right good shock when he come back up to us carryin a shotgun.

He dumped a sack and a unlit lantern next to where Pa lay, then said, "Don't you worry your head, Golden Lea. I tole Masta I was gonna hunt him up some possum for tomorrow's supper. Masta's right fond of possum, but he's too lazy to hunt at night. Claims he needs his sleep. Now, let's git your pa up. We gotta git outta sight fore I light this lantern."

It weren't no easy task, but tween the two of us we moved Pa to the other side of the hill. Then Silas lit the lantern and checked Pa's wound.

"This here has gotta be cut open to let the pus out," he said. "Elsewise, your pa ain't gonna live to see Ohio. That's a sure fact." He stopped long enough to look at me. "Ohio's where y'all are goin, right?"

"Yes, sir."

"Well, the good part is that y'all are only bout ten miles from the Ohio River. But you gotta be mighty careful, Golden Lea. Them patrollers is all round that river. Whatever you do, *don't try crossin the Ohio in daylight. You gotta find yourself a boat and git across at night. And you ain't gonna be safe jus cause you git to the other side. The law says you can be sent back wherever you're caught, in slave territory or free."*

I didn't say nothin and Silas commenced to runnin his knife through the flame on the lantern. "What's your pa's name?" he asked.

"Elijah."

Silas leaned over to put his face in front of Pa's, so that Pa couldn't help but see him. "Elijah, can you hear me?"

Pa looked at Silas for a minute, his eyes blinkin like they was fulla sand. Then he said, "Yessum, I hears you."

"I gotta cut that wound open, Elijah. Iffen I don't, you'll die for sure. But the thing is, you need to stay quiet. You reckon you can do that?"

Pa's head come up, the look in his eye so wild I leaned away. But he was firm, despite his fever. "Y'all do what you gotta."

Silas's hand was swift and the blade of his knife cut deep. What come outta that wound, the blood and the pus, was surely the ugliest mess I ever seen. Pa's face twisted in agony when Silas squeezed the wound, but he didn't make no sound more than a low grunt. Me, I thought it would never end, but Silas finally did stop. He dabbed the wound with a salve he says was made of bear fat and snakeroot, then wrapped it round with a piece of rag. And Pa, he jus fell back and stared up at the sky.

"I gotta go hunt a possum," Silas said, "or Masta will be right unhappy come mornin. Golden Lea, you bout the bravest little girl I ever laid eyes on. If you was my child, I'd be real proud. But you got the hardest part still ahead. Have somethin

to eat, then git your pa on his feet and start travelin north. He won't git no better stayin here."

Silas walked away into the woods then. And though I never laid eyes on that man again, I carry his face round in my head to this very day. I spect Silas helped us outta pure charity, but charity don't splain him, not altogether. Many a man has seen others in trouble and turned away cause they was scared to help. But Silas, he took a real risk when he stole that bag of food. Peoples like his mistriss and masta, what live close to the bone, keeps track of the food.

I don't knowed if any harm came to Silas later on, but I was right glad for what he carried in that sack. There was bread and cheese and pickled eggs and a jar of blackberry preserves. I pushed Pa to eat and drink, pushed him hard, but I didn't have to push to git him movin. Bout an hour after Silas left, Pa took up his walkin stick and climbed to his feet. He didn't say nothin to me, jus gathered his strength for a minute, and drew a deep breath. Then we went on.

Chapter 12

FAMILY AND FAITH

THEY TOOK THE feeding tube out at nine o'clock the next morning. Trust me, this was no fun. The tube had to be two feet long and it came up through my throat and out my nose, leaving a raw, burning pain along the way. But I was glad to see it go. Being fed through a tube wasn't all that appetizing, either.

I was better in other ways, too. I started to talk again. The words came slowly and haltingly, and there were times when I had to find substitutes for the words I heard in my head. Like, if I wanted to say the word *find*, but couldn't get it out, I'd use the word *discover* instead. Weird. It was like I swallowed a thesaurus.

I wasn't off the hook with the infection, either. Dr. Balder made that very clear when he showed up around ten o'clock. Yes, the most severe symptoms had diminished, partly due to the antibiotics and partly due to the surgery. But the fluids draining through the tube in my brain still contained bacteria when they should have been sterile. My kidney functions were also weak, although he felt they'd improve as the infection diminished. I'd need another MRI that day to see how things were progressing. And for the next few days, at the very least, I would have to remain in the hospital, so I shouldn't get my hopes up all that much. But hope was all I had.

Ah, that Dr. Balder. Always full of good news. Still, staying in the hospital was fine with me. I was still so weak that I had no desire to be anywhere but in that bed with my eyes glued to the television bracketed on the wall. I watched the morning shows, the talk shows, and the soaps in the afternoon. I had a sense that nothing more was required of me. Good or bad, my body was doing its own thing. And without much help from me, thank you very much.

For a while, that whole staying in bed, watching TV thing was actually cool. Imagine a sick day from school when you didn't really feel that bad, just tired. And you knew you weren't going to have to go to school the next day or probably the day after that, so homework was, like, the last thing on your mind. Most kids could really get into that, right? For a few days, at least. Without going totally crazy with boredom. I admit a Wii would have helped. But, for now, it would have to be me and Oprah and *All My Children*. My parents probably hoped that I wasn't getting too used to the lifestyle. At home, I was only allowed an hour of television a day.

Mom and Dad stayed by my side for the entire morning, just as they had the night before. They looked almost as tired as I felt, and for the most part we maintained a silence. I can't speak for my parents, but even aside from the problem I had forming words, I didn't feel much need for conversation. I felt so tightly bound to both my mother and father by then that we might have been a single organism. No words were necessary to express our feelings.

Kids rarely think about family ties. That's because they take their parents' love for granted. Worse yet, they demand more of it whenever they can. *Yo, gimme some more of that.* But I was going in another direction now. I was finally realizing that no one else on the entire planet would turn their lives upside down to care for me the way they had. Nobody else would exhaust the last drop of their energies on my behalf, or sit around in the same clothes, day after day, eating cafeteria slop and hanging on every word the doctors and nurses said.

Nobody. Can you hear me now? There are six-and-a-half billion people on this planet and I could only count on two of them to really watch my back. I mean, like, *every second.* Talk about a limited circle of protection. There are lots of really, really bad things that can happen to you in your lifetime (trust me on this), but only a very small number of people who'll be there for you if one of those bad things should land on your head with both feet. Those people are your family. You know, the ones we're usually fighting with, or yelling at, or complaining to our friends about.

I know there's supposed to be a gulf between gratitude and love. But is there a difference between care and love? I didn't think so. Not anymore. Care is the outward expression of love, in my opinion. If my parents weren't able to speak—if they were stricken with silence for a few hours the way I had been—I still would've heard them loud and clear. They loved me, and because of that, they took care of me. It was as simple and yet as profound as all that.

While I was lying there, watching TV, there was some talk of me going home in a few days if I continued to improve and if the MRI came back all right. Improve? In a few days? Gimme a break. I could barely get out of bed. Heck, I could hardly change the channels when a commercial came on! Without my parents to care for me when I got home, I wouldn't be able to care for myself. I was completely dependent for the time being. And you know what? For such an independent young lady, it didn't bother me nearly as much as I would've imagined. They loved me, so they took care of me. Nothing to be embarrassed about. In fact, I felt pretty proud.

But something strange did occur. I noticed that the thought of going home scared me a bit. Before, it was like, *Whoo-hoo! I get to go home. TTYL, hospital. Talk to you later—or hopefully never.*

Now, as I looked around the room, I took an inventory of the medical instruments on the wall, the machines around my bed. How would I survive at home without them? Who would do all the work that the doctors, and the nurses, and the hospital staff kept up around the clock?

An orderly came into the room just then, an elderly black man with a white cloth hanging out of his back pocket, who groaned when he bent over to change the plastic bag lining the wastebasket. The television over the bed was on, but I wasn't listening. My attention was focused on an obvious truth, something I should have figured out a long time ago. Love begins with care. My parents would take care of me and protect me the best they could, it's true. But these strangers at the hospital? They did an amazing job, too. Not because they loved me in particular, but because they loved helping people in whatever way they could. Selfless love. It was like Silas had done in the last few pages that my mom had read to me and like what Golden Lea had told me in my dream: Love people the way you want to be loved, and that meant looking out for each other.

I smiled at the man taking out my garbage and told him, "Thank you."

I guess I dozed off after that, because when I opened my eyes again, it was an hour later, and Daddy was peeling back the wrapper of a Snickers bar. Three containers of coffee sat in their styrofoam containers on the tray table and I watched my mother drink from one. That was another thing. At home, Mom rarely drank more than one cup of coffee or tea. She had enough energy for two people without the caffeine. Now she was knocking down a quart of hospital coffee every day. And, let me tell you, that stuff didn't look all that tempting. It was kind of grayish-brown, like the color of snow on the side of the highway.

"Mom?" I said softly.

"Maddie, you're awake."

Mom's face appeared over the edge of the bed, followed by Daddy's. Their looks were concerned. Maybe they thought I was about to utter my final words. If they were, they weren't going to be all that deep. Nothing for the history books, unfortunately.

"Mom, I feel like I escaped from…" I could hear the word *prison* in my head, clear as glass, but I couldn't get it out. Finally, I settled for, "I feel like I escaped from… jail."

"What do you mean?" She looked at me quizzically, stroking my head.

"When I first got sick, I felt…trapped," I said. "Now, I feel like I learned a lot. Like I have fewer limitations. Only… only I feel…" The word I wanted was *sorry*. I felt sorry for my mom and dad. For everything they went through. But I gave up; it was out of my reach. "I feel bad…"

"You feel bad? Sick? Want me to call the doctor?" She said all this in a quick rush of words. Naturally, Mom got it wrong. So, what's new? But at least she was trying.

"No. I feel bad for you and Dad," I managed.

"Baby, you can't blame yourself. Your illness isn't your fault."

See? What did I tell you? Family. They don't give a second thought to their sacrifices. I smiled weakly at my mother. "Did you bring Golden Lea's…journal?" I asked.

"There's only a few more pages, baby, and I left the book at home."

I sighed. Enough with the *baby* already. Okay, I accepted that I was pretty helpless at that point and completely dependent on doctors, parents, and pretty much every medical machine known to man. But I wasn't a baby. Babies didn't have any experience of the world. I, however, had pretty much been through it all.

Josh said that having a brain tumor changes you and he was absolutely right. I wasn't a baby anymore. I wasn't even a kid. I was fourteen going on four hundred. But that didn't mean I was above whining to get my way.

"Mommy, could you get it, please?" I pleaded. "I mean, I'm being…wheelchaired away for another MRI soon. If it goes like the last one, I'll be in radiology for a couple of… for a long time."

How could she resist?

My parents left a short time later to get the book. To be honest, I think they were grateful for a chance to get away. A change of clothes and a long shower was what they needed anyway. I would have told them to stay home for the rest of the day if I thought there was any chance they'd agree.

For me, however, the medication merry-go-round was once again in full gear, before and after my parents left. So it wasn't like I was exactly left alone. Every hour or so, a nurse appeared bearing some pill, or liquid, or a syringe. I asked one of them why I couldn't take everything at one time and got the usual condescending reply.

"Doctor's orders, dear."

Fine, fine. It broke up the day, anyway.

But it didn't end there. I think I gave blood five times that morning. My arms looked like bruised pincushions, and I sort of promised myself I'd lay off the vampire movies and books when I got home. All that blood was about as tempting as the hospital coffee.

But not even the sight of yet another syringe, or the two hours I'd spend waiting for my MRI in the intensive care unit, could break the prevailing mood. Which was overall pretty glum. I didn't ask what the blood was for. I didn't ask why I couldn't have remained in my own room until the MRI lab was ready for me. I knew by now that this was all part of the routine, and the hospital personnel—from the brain surgeons, to the aides who made my bed, to the orderlies who cleaned my room—were all mechanics. Their mission was to repair broken machines, and my machine (while hopefully not wrecked beyond repair) was definitely broken. I have to admit, though, that the routine was becoming kind of played out at this point.

Lunch was waiting for me on the little rolling table by my bed when I came back up from radiology. Not exactly what you'd call a welcome sight: a small bowl of soup, a little package of soda crackers, and a container of melted ice cream. I drank the ice cream, but the soup—cream of some vegetable still to be identified—was beyond me. I was pouring it out down the sink when Josh Grappinelli showed up. He took a couple of steps into the room, then stopped and shook his head.

"Nurse," he said, "put her back in the cage. She's escaped again."

I hobbled back to bed as fast as I could, holding the back of the hospital gown closed with one hand for modesty's sake, and pushing the IV stand ahead of me with the other.

"You're supposed to…announce yourself," I declared, sounding quite a bit more formal than I had intended to.

"Male in the room," he grinned.

"Too little, too late," I kidded.

"Oh, man, that is so old school. Besides, the door was open." Josh came up to the bed and we exchanged a quick fist bump. "So," he said, "how ya doin'?"

"Ghetto fabulous?" I tried.

"Still the tough guy," Josh said. "Why am I not surprised?"

"Check it out, bro, attitude is…" I wanted to say *everything*, but had to settle for *important*, which sounded pretty dumb.

"Seriously, Maddie, what's the story? Why are you still here?"

"I developed an infection and it had to be cleaned out. Now I'm having trouble with my words." I found that I could relate to Josh the way two veterans of the same war could relate to each other. With my parents, I felt constricted. Their fears were obvious and I was never sure if they were withholding information. But Josh had been through it all and had come out the other side. Plus, he had the battle scars to prove it.

I just shrugged, unable to say anymore about my condition. "How about you?" I asked, concerned. He looked just as skinny and just as worn out as the first time I saw him, maybe more so. "How are you?"

"Same old, same old. I'm in for a radiation treatment," he answered evenly.

"I might be headed down that… lane. What are they like, radiation and…" Unfortunately, there wasn't another word for "chemotherapy" and I just left the sentence dangling.

Josh got the point, despite the lapse. "Chemo? Chemo drugs are poisons and poisons make you sick. The hope is that they'll kill the cancer without killing you first. Radiation isn't much better. Fatigue? Brain swelling? Skin inflammation? Hair loss? Depression? I mean, what's not to like?"

I smiled because the joke was pretty funny, even though the answer wasn't. Then we were silent for a moment, and I let my head drop back on the pillow and listened to the IV pump as it clicked away. The television was on, too, but the volume was down, so that the figures on the screen yapped away soundlessly.

A boy no more than eight years old passed by my door, accompanied by two adults. The boy wore pinstriped pajamas with the Yankees logo on the chest. The side of his head, like my own, was heavily bandaged.

Watching him walk by, I said, "The depression part is what worries me the most. I mean, I have an option. Dr. Balder says my tumor is benign and it grows…not very fast. I could decide to watch and wait."

I was sorry for the words as soon as I said them. Benign? Slow growing? Watch and wait? Josh's position was so much worse than mine. What right did I have to complain? But Josh only nodded. Trust me when I tell you that he was a trooper.

"I know what you mean about depression," he said. "But you can't let it take over your life. I mean, what would be the point in that? Who wants to live that way?"

Another silence, this time because I felt suddenly exhausted. The MRI and all the tests had stripped me of energy and my batteries were definitely run down. If I had been a smoke alarm, I would be beeping.

I took one last look at Josh then let my eyes close. I drifted for a while, halfway between sleep and wakefulness, and my thoughts gradually turned to my ancestor, Golden Lea Jackson. Golden Lea looked to God every time she ran into trouble. No matter what happened, her faith was unshaken. Meanwhile, I'd been raised to overcome problems through my own efforts. I didn't ask God to help me get good grades. I studied. I didn't ask God to help me win basketball games. I practiced. Kids, what do they know except what their parents tell them? Mom was a big-time overcomer, the can-do gal personified. In his own way, my dad was the same. Quiet and low-key, he projected a competence that was impossible to challenge, even when he was wrong. Which, to my knowledge, wasn't often.

I opened my eyes to find Josh still there, sitting beside the bed. Who knows how long he was waiting there? I had again lost track of time.

"Do you believe in God?" I asked suddenly.

"Absolutely," he said.

"Do you pray?"

"Oh, yeah," he grinned. "I was raised in an old-fashioned Baptist family. We pray a lot."

"What do you pray for?"

"Mostly, I don't pray to ask for anything. I pray to give thanks."

Thanks? I thought. *Thanks for what?* But I kind of knew the answer. Thanks for the time he has with his family. Thanks for each day he opens his eyes. I sort of felt the same way.

The next question I wanted to approach rather delicately. "Do you pray that you'll get…that you'll recover?"

"No, Maddie, I really don't," he said calmly.

"Why not?"

He leaned back in his chair and stared down at his hands for a minute. Then he looked straight into my eyes and said, "The survival rate for my cancer is fifty percent after five years. So, if I ask God to include me in the survivor category, it seems like I'm also asking Him to put somebody else on the other end of the equation."

Whoa. "It's not…sinful to want to live," I protested. I didn't want Josh giving up. Ever.

"Don't get me wrong, tough guy. I haven't asked my folks to put a down payment on my coffin just yet." Josh smiled a crooked smile as he scratched at the rash on his scalp. "But I just can't believe that God would listen to a prayer that asked Him to choose between Josh Grappinelli and some other kid. So, I don't really put Him in that position. It's like asking a mutual friend to take sides when you and your best friend get into a big argument."

Now what middle school kid couldn't relate to that?

"So I don't pray for anything in particular," Josh continued. "I pray for others, for my family, and I give Him props."

"Then why do you pray at all?"

"Praying makes me feel good. No, forget that. Praying makes me feel peaceful. It makes me feel close to God. The very act itself produces its own reward, like a peace that endures…"

At least until the next chemo treatment, I thought. But I let that one go.

"Do you ever get depressed?" I asked.

"Yeah, sometimes. The fatigue alone is enough to get you down, you know? It means I can't spend whatever time I have left doing the things I love. Sports. Going out with my friends. Forget it. And my chemo will go on for at least another year, so I'm not gonna get healthy any time soon. But that's just the way it is. Life doesn't come with a guarantee."

"Yeah," I agreed.

That's pretty close to what Golden Lea said in my dream. Not quite "Live each moment like it's your last." Too depressing. More like "Live each moment like it's a gift."

"Josh," I said.

"Yeah?"

"You're not so bad…for a kid from Bensonhurst."

My parents came back at around four o'clock, a short time after Josh had left. I was kind of glad that they had missed each other. Didn't want them to think we were going steady.

Happily, Mom was bearing a white paper bag. Inside the bag was a chocolate milkshake from Checker's drive-in. My favorite. I didn't know I was hungry until I saw that container. Then I was suddenly ravenous.

"I got the okay from Dr. Balder before we left," she said with a wink.

As I drank the milkshake, I had a sudden revelation. I'd lost a good ten pounds over the last few days. Now I'd have to gain them back. Can you say, *Happy days are here again?* It was like a license to eat junk food! Josh was right. Who wants to sit around being depressed when there are milkshakes to drink?

An hour later, it was time for dinner. Two thin slices of turkey, overcooked mashed potatoes (without gravy), a piece of gray bread, and a little bowl of chocolate pudding that might have been scooped from the La Brea Tar Pits. Boy, what I wouldn't do for another gourmet treat from the Checker's drive-in instead! Oh, well. I didn't want to put the whole ten pounds back on all in one day. I ate the whole mess so fast—hoping my taste buds wouldn't have a chance to catch up—that I was still burping an hour later when I fell asleep.

It was nine o'clock when I woke up. Mom and Dad were in their usual positions, sitting in the armchairs by my bed. Mom was reading through some legal papers and Dad was lost in a mystery novel that he bought at the hospital's gift shop. It looked like a scene straight out of our living room—and suddenly, I was homesick.

I closed my eyes for a minute, thinking you really don't know how precious life is until you've been close to death. Moments like this, when Dad wasn't jetting off to Greece and Mom wasn't working overtime in the office, were what I was truly thankful for. Okay, so it didn't have to be in a hospital, but I understood what Josh was talking about: I was lucky.

Then I thought of Golden Lea, too, and of my dream. She told me I had to go back, that I had work to do. I wondered how long it would take me to find out what that work was—and I thought of all the options that were hopefully still in front of me. They were opportunities Golden Lea didn't have, despite her good health.

"Mom," I finally said, "tell me what you think about Golden Lea's story. I mean, it's one thing to read a novel about slavery, or even a true…tale about someone who isn't related. But this is your…forebear. Mine, too. We were once slaves."

Mom looked up from her papers. "Except for African immigrants, Maddie, almost every black person you meet is descended from someone who came to this part of the world on a slave ship. That's just as true for the Caribbean or South America as for the United States."

I knew this, of course, but something had changed now. Slavery wasn't, like, the *past*. It wasn't just *American history* anymore. It was something that had happened to someone in my family. It was personal.

"What do you think about that, Daddy? You're married to someone whose ancestors were slaves."

My father never speaks off the top of his head, especially when he's asked a loaded question like that one. Finally, he said, "It's not just slavery. Slavery was bad enough, but what happened after the slaves were freed—the lingering racism—is also a betrayal to humanity. Your mother and I had to get past that and, believe me, it wasn't easy." He reached out and took Mom's hand. "As for my ancestors, my excuse is that for most of that time during slavery, they were busy stomping grapes in the mountains of Sicily."

I knew, at that point, that I wasn't going to get a straight answer from either of them. Maybe that was for the best. Maybe they didn't know what to make of it themselves.

I closed my eyes again, contemplating my own question and how *I* felt about Golden Lea's story. But before I knew it, I fell asleep once more. Such was my busy social schedule.

I woke up again around one o'clock in the morning. The overhead light was out and the only illumination in the room came from a dim nightlight behind the bed. Mom and Dad were both asleep in the reclining armchairs.

For a time, I simply lay there and listened to the hospital sounds. They weren't anything like the sounds of nature that you hear when you're camping out under the stars, but they'd have to do for now. The clicking of the IV pump and the occasional blip of a heart monitor. A blood pressure cuff wrapped around my left arm suddenly inflated then released its air with a sharp hiss. I heard voices out by the nurses' station and a burst of laughter. The laughter stopped abruptly when an alarm beeped on the other side of the unit.

I looked over at Mom and Dad. Still asleep. Very slowly, feeling like I might pass out at any moment, I sat up and slid my feet over the side of the bed. Mom's purse—large enough to qualify for oversized luggage on an airline flight—was sitting next to her chair. I managed to bend over far enough to reach the strap, then I pulled it toward me and started to rummage around inside as quietly as I could. Success! A moment later, I was staring at my face in the mirror of her compact. The light was dim, but I could see well enough. In fact, I think the dimmer the light, the better.

At first, I barely recognized the face in the mirror as my own. It didn't help that I was making that quivering, just-about-to-cry face that never looks good on anyone except a few well-practiced Hollywood actresses. I closed my eyes to stop the tears and took a couple of deep, calming breaths.

Then I opened my eyes and looked again. After I got over my initial horror, I started laughing. I mean, talk about a mess! An Oprah makeover wouldn't have repaired the damage.

The drainage tube jutting from my scalp looked like a tentacle and one side of my head was so swollen that my face might have been assembled from the faces of two different people. Talk about a Phantom-of-the-Opera moment! Maybe I could find a job in a Coney Island house of horrors. Was that the "work" Golden Lea was talking about? Because in addition to the tube and the swelling, my eyes were rimmed by circles so dark that it looked like I'd been wearing cheap mascara in a rainstorm!

So, why was this girl in the mirror laughing? I was laughing because, as I stared at myself more and more, I realized that it didn't matter what I looked like. It never really mattered. At that moment, I was just glad to be alive.

My laughter woke Mom up. She saw me staring into the mirror and said the first word that came into her mind: "Baby…"

"Not again with the baby thing," I said, rolling my eyes.

Mom cleared her throat and tried again. "*Maddie*, are you okay?"

"Yeah, I'm doing fine. For a space alien." I handed Mom back the compact.

Mom smiled at the joke in spite of herself. "Wait, I've brought something for you," she added excitedly.

Mom rummaged in her purse and I expected her to pull out Golden Lea's book. Trust me, it was roomy enough for ten copies. Instead, she came up with a worn photograph.

"This is a photo of Golden Lea," Mom said. "It was taken when she was very old. I thought you might like to see it."

The photograph was in bad shape. The paper was yellowed and crackled and the image was faded. The photographer had made an amateur mistake, too. Golden Lea was facing away from a sunlit background and her face was deeply shadowed. But it didn't matter. I recognized her instantly from my dream: the filmy eyes, the short, broad nose and high cheekbones, the no-nonsense mouth, the white apron over a gingham dress.

Yep, that was Golden Lea all right, in all her glory. Looking proud and unbroken, despite what life had handed her.

My own eyes instantly welled up and I leaned back against the pillow. That girl laughing in the mirror a moment ago? I guess she was just a baby in some respects because she had had it easy all her life. She had Mommy and Daddy beside her, a warm place to sleep at night and enough food to keep her full. And all this was even true *in a hospital.*

I wanted to tell Mom, and Dad, too, right then how much I loved them, and how grateful I felt. This time, I couldn't find the right words because there *weren't any* to express exactly how much they meant to me. All I could do was take Mom's hand. She understood well enough what I was trying to tell her, though. I'm sure of this because she was crying, too.

Eventually, Mom put the photo away and took out Golden Lea's *Recollections.*

"You ready?" she asked, no hesitation about reading the dialect now.

I took a deep breath and closed my eyes. "For anything."

Chapter 13

A HARD-FOUGHT FREEDOM

T HE FOG COME up a short time after the sun went down and the night was very dark in the valleys. This was good for keepin us hid—at times the mist was so thick I could barely see the trees ahead—but it made for slow goin.

For a time, we followed a stream that run north. There were bats over the stream. What they was up to, I can't say. What I can say is they come swoopin and turnin outta the fog so fast I thought sure they was gonna run smack into my face. I couldn't see em till they wasn't no more than a few feet away and I figured they couldn't see me, neither. But they never did crash into me or Pa. Jus twisted and turned, comin outta the mist and vanishin back fore I could do more than blink my eye.

When the stream turned east, we started into a pine forest. Pine makes for easier walkin on accounta brush don't grow beneath it. But the way got steeper still and the ground underfoot was treacherous with shale and loose rock. I was deathly afraid Pa was gonna fall and not be able to git up. I was jus a girl and not built big and I knew I couldn't carry him.

We walked on without talkin. I was at the furthermost point of my energies and I didn't have no thoughts in my head cept puttin one foot down, then the other, then do it over again. Ol Silas said the Ohio River weren't more than ten miles to the north and I kep hopin to see it from every ridge we crossed that night. The ridge lines was above the fog, which hung heavy in the valleys, and what I saw ahead, for most of that night, was another ridge line risin outta the mist like the blade of an axe.

The moon was full and its light turned the fog into silver rivers that seemed to run on and on forever. Me and Pa stopped to eat when the moon was straight overhead. We stopped down in one of the valleys, where the fog kep us hidden, right near a stream that leapt lively along a rocky bed. Pa didn't sit, jus leaned with his back against a tree and took the weight off his foot. I spected he was afraid he wouldn't be able to git back up iffen he sat down, but I didn't say nothin. I scooped water and took it to him and watched him drink. His eyes was all hollow and bright with fever.

"Daughter," he said, "I needs to hear you say somethin."

"Say what, Pa?"

"I needs to hear you say you are goin on, no matter what happens to me."

"Don't be talkin like that. That there is givin up. Silas said it weren't more than ten miles to the river and we near mos there, so I don't want to hear one more word."

My voice surprised me as much as it did Pa. I was never one to sass my elders and here I was scoldin my own pa. But I couldn't listen to no more talk bout goin on alone. Jus thinkin bout it caused my heart to ache.

"Whyn't you eat somethin, Pa?"

I handed up a hunk of bread slathered with blackberry preserves and a piece of cheese. He nibbled at the bread, but didn't hardly git but a few crumbs down. I watched him struggle, seein the pain in his eyes, and I had a moment of darkness when I wished them all dead, every slaveholdin dog among em. First they took my mama away from me and now they was near to killin my pa. These was dirty deeds, but they was never to suffer for it on this Earth. No, sir. When he was havin his fancy parties, Masta Harris put more food on the table than a slave eats in a year. His carriage was gilded and the seats inside was soft as feather cushions. But his slaves didn't have no more than a dirt floor and a corn-shuck mattress and the chirrens ate from a trough.

Why would the Lord make a world like that? Seems like the worstest peoples had everythin and the bestest peoples didn't have nothin. They didn't have nothin and they wouldn't git nothin, no matter how hard they worked. And their chirrens wouldn't have nothin, neither. A Christian is sposed to trust in the Lord, but I was plumb outta trust. I listened to a bobcat scream out in the distance. The sound come through the fog and cut into me, a sharp and lonesome cry. Then I rememba the words spoke by Jesus on the Mount:

Ye have heard it hath been said, Thou shalt love thy neighbor and hate thine enemy. But I say to you, Love your enemies, bless them that curse you, do good to them that hate you, and them which use you for spite and persecute you, that you may be the children of your Father which is in heaven.

I realized then that lovin your enemies wasn't somethin you could jus do, like fetchin wood to make a fire. Uh-uh. Lovin God? That wasn't no way hard. Lovin folks like Masta Harris

177

and Missy Ann was an entirely different thing. I might take my whole life and never git it done. But I gotta try.

"Pa," I said, "why does the Lord allow mens like Masta Harris to whip mens and womens who never did nothin to deserve it? Iffen I was the Lord, I would put a stop to mistreatin innocent folks in a big hurry."

Pa didn't answer right then. He pushed a few more crumbs into his mouth and chewed on em till I thought he'd chew right through his teeth. Then he took up his walkin stick from where it lay against a tree.

"I think I done tole you," he said, "that my daddy was took from Africa when he was a young man."

"You tole me that he was from a people called the Benin."

"That's right. That's what he said. Anyways, he finally become a Christian after bein here a long time, but the religion he was raised in as a boy was different. His folk believe in spirits, some of em good and some of em bad. The bad spirits, they would git into peoples and run em like they was some kinda contraption. I reckon that's what happened to Masta Harris."

"Christians don't believe in them kind of spirits." I tole him. "That's how I was taught."

From off in the far distance, a dog started into barkin. Me and Pa froze as hard as the icicles hangin off Masta's porch in the winter. But the dog stopped after a minute and the only sound was the sound of the stream over the rocks.

"My daddy," Pa said, "claimed that angels and demons was how Christians talked bout spirits. He said Masta Harris and his like have been claimed by demons, same as if they was under a spell. They been tricked by the devil into believin they's

right in what they does. Tha's how come Masta can go to his church on Sundays and pray to the Lord. He thinks he's goin to heaven, but he's in for a big surprise."

I thought bout this for a minute. It surely made sense to me right then, but it didn't answer my question. "I understands that, Pa, and I understands that when Masta Harris faces judgment, the devil will claim his own. But I don't see why the Lord lets it go on."

Pa finally took a step, then another. "I believe since Silas cut my leg, I'm feelin a might better. Leastwise, it don't hurt much no more. Now let's git goin. Iffen Silas was right, we should be wadin in the Ohio River fore sunrise."

I gathered up the bag and slung it over my shoulder. I was figurin I wouldn't git no answer, but Pa spoke over his shoulder as he started up the hill. "One day, y'all will be standin fore the Lord. Then you can ask Him your own self. For now, for the time ya'll on this Earth, you jus gotta deal with what's out there."

Pa was wrong bout us wadin in the Ohio River that night. When we finally come up on the river, we was on a bluff, lookin down a coupla hundred feet at the water. Now the Ohio River ain't no ocean. It ain't even the Mississippi River. But it was the mos water this girl ever seen and I knowed right away that I could never swim across. We was gonna have to find us a boat.

The fog had gathered on both banks, but the river was clear and the moonlight was splashed over the still waters. I couldn't see nothin of what farms might be on either bank, but I knowed they had to be there. And I knowed, too, that whoever lived on them farms had boats. There was fish to catch in those waters and the river was better than any road for gettin crops to market.

I think I coulda stood there till doomsday, jus watchin the river, but I had Pa to see to. He took one look at the river and smiled. Then he backed off into the trees and lay down. Didn't seem like a minute till he was sleepin. Pa's sleep wasn't quiet, not no way. He started in to sweatin and talkin out loud. I couldn't make no sense of the words and I jus covered him with the blanket. I wanted to tend his wound, only it was too dark, so I soaked one corner of the blanket and lay it cross his head. Lands, that man was so hot the blanket come near to givin off steam.

Worries and worries. I found me a spot between two trees where I could look out over the water at the bluffs on the other side. The stars was sparklin in the heavens and the moon was hangin off to the west. That's when I seen the boat for the first time. It poked outta the fog on the Kentucky side, ridin near to the bank as it moved upstream. I could see a man at the oars, very faint, and there was folks in fronta and behind him. The boat continued on for a ways, keepin close to the shadows, then suddenly turned across the river. Even from where I was, I could see how hard the man was rowin. That boat jus bout flew over the water fore it disappeared in the mist.

I sat right where I was, watchin and hopin. Sure enough, not more than fifteen minutes later, the boat come back empty save for the man at the oars.

Gradually the moon went down till it hung on one horizon jus as the tip of the sun showed on the other. The birds commenced to singin in the trees all round and the mist along the banks of the Ohio River turned pink at the top. I heard sounds from the farms below, cattle bellowin, roosters crowin, an axe choppin into wood. Bit by bit, the mist rose up, becomin thinner and thinner till it was gone altogether.

What emerged below weren't exactly encouragin. There was farms coverin mos of the flatland on either side of the river, with only patches of forest between em. The boat I seen had come from one patch that ran straight back from the river to the bluff, like a tongue of the forest reachin out to the water for a long drink. A good ways off to the east, a town was laid out in rows of buildins, some of em brick. Smoke was risin outta chimneys and there was a wharf leadin into the river with boats tied up to it. A few of em boats was large and had sails, a coupla em was flat for haulin wagons and teams, and one of em was a steamboat. I watched the steamboat pull away from the wharf, backin into the river, then turnin to the west, away from where I was sittin. This was the first steamboat I ever seen and I couldn't turn my eyes away till it rounded a bend in the river and disappeared.

All through that mornin, boats came and went from the town wharf. Mosly, they headed west, toward the Mississippi River, which I didn't knowed at the time. I was jus glad they wasn't comin in my direction cause I knew, come nightfall, me and Pa was gonna have to sneak down into that patch of woods. I was hopin the man who rowed that boat cross the river would come back again, but even iffen he didn't, me and Pa would use that boat to gain our freedom. This was stealin, I knowed, and I hoped the Lord would forgive me. Iffen I'd seen another way, I woulda took it.

I fell asleep for a spell with my back against the tree. The sun was straight overhead by the time I opened my eyes and my first thought was of my pa. I jumped up quick and rushed *over to where he was lyin. Pa was in the worse shape so far. His fever was high and his breath was rattlin away in his chest. I lifted him half-up till he was sittin with his back against a big rock and he commenced to coughin up gobs of bloody phlegm. I gave him water and it seemed to ease him some. Still, I was bout as scared as I could git.*

"We ain't got far to go, Pa," I said. "Come night, we gonna git cross the river to free country. We gonna be free."

I didn't wait for Pa to say nothin. I was too scared he'd talk bout leavin me again. So I jumped right into what I seen the night fore. I tole him bout the man in the boat and his passengers and how the man snuck down through the mist and how the boat come back empty.

"That boat is tied up in them woods right now, Pa. All we gotta do is wait for dark."

Pa's eyes turned full on me and I seen hope in em. He commenced to crawl forward toward the edge of the bluff. When he got to where he could see the river, he layed flat on his stomach and looked out. There were quite a number of boats on the water, mosly under sail, and the farms was real busy, too. That come as no surprise on accounta it was late summer and the crops was near to ripe.

"The boat is in them woods right there." I waited till he nodded his head. "There ain't no reason why we can't walk along the bluff till we directly above it, then work our way down."

"Girl, you done right good, but I would sure like to knows what happened to them folks when they got off on the other side of the river. Iffen there's help out there, we'd be blessed by the Lord to find it."

"Well, this time, we gonna give the Lord some help. Come night, we gonna climb down through them woods and find

us that boat. Then we gonna wait. Iffen that man show up, we'll cross with em. Iffen he don't, we'll cross on our own jus fore dawn."

That day was bout the longest of my life. There weren't nothin to do but watch the boats on the river and the little clouds as they floated over the sky. The sun was almost down fore the farmers and their field hands went in for dinner. I was hopin that would be the end of em, but a little later, a few come out with poles, includin some boys, and commenced to fishin. The moon was up, but still low on the horizon to the east. I spose it throwed enough light for the mens to see what they was doin. But then the fog formed along the river's banks, north and south, and the fishermens quit and headed home.

"Bout time, I do believe." Pa slid back into the woods and rose to his feet. He was mos shaky and his breathin was still poor. For jus a minute, I thought he was gonna fall right back on his face. Then he straightened up.

"Don't you worry, Pa. You gonna be all right."

"That ain't up to me, Golden Lea. Nor to you, neither. Now let's git on our way."

Maybe Pa was right. Maybe the future weren't up to me. But that didn't stop me from prayin to the man in charge. Me and Pa made our way east, keepin the edge of the bluff in sight. Twice, I heard some animal skitter through the woods, but iffen there was another human bein in them hills, I didn't see nor hear em.

Eventually, we come to where the woods run straight down the side of the bluff all the way to the river. Pa, he didn't try to walk down that hill. It was too steep. He slid down on his bottom, comin slow and careful, stoppin again and again to listen. There was farms on either side of them woods, but all was quiet.

When we finally got to level ground, we come up against a problem I hadn't figured on. The first thing I had to do was find that boat, only the fog was so thick I coulda shaped it into corn mush. I left Pa to go searchin—I didn't have no choice—but when I found the boat, I had trouble findin Pa again. And when I finally got Pa on his feet, I had to wander round for a good ten minutes fore I come on that boat again.

By the time we settled down, my heart was beatin hard in my chest. Ol Jack Trembley had scared me right to my bones when he come on us in the woods. This was different. This was bein scared of things you can't see. This was bein scared that jus when you was real close to gettin everythin, you might lose it all in a minute. And we was in right poor condition, too. Pa could barely walk and I was scratched and scraped and bit all over my body. My dress was torn near to bein a rag.

It got to where I started thinkin if anythin else went wrong I wouldn't have no strength to resist. Then I heard them dogs. Right away I seen it was different from when the farm dogs would start barkin. Fact, these dogs wasn't barkin a'tall. They was bayin, like dogs on the hunt. The sound was sharp in the still air and it seemed to be comin from everywhere at the same time, like we was surrounded. I was in such a panic, I started runnin in circles.

"Pa, Pa, git up," I says. "The patrollers is comin and we gotta use the boat."

Pa tried to rise on his own. He put his weight on his good foot and got himself to one knee. Then he jus fell over. I ran to him and yanked on his arms, pullin with all the strength in my body and prayin prayers like I never prayed, fore or since.

When Pa was finally standin up, I laid his arms cross my shoulder and we started for the boat. But it weren't no good.

The boat was a good twenty feet from the river, hid in the brush, and I couldn't move it but a few inches. Pa tried to help, but he was so weak he fell back down.

"You go on, Golden Lea. Quick, fore them dogs git on ya."

The dogs was closer now and their bayin seemed to churn the fog. I didn't have no idea what to do. I couldn't leave my pa, but I knew, sure as the sunrise, that iffen we was took, we would be whipped hard and then sold off, never to see each other again. I started pushin on that boat again, rockin it from side to side, then shovin at the back, cryin my eyes out till I couldn't see nothin beyond my own tears. I wanted to give up and jus wait for whatever was gonna happen. I could hear footsteps now, runnin footsteps, and they was comin straight for us.

I grabbed hold of Pa, but even fore I could lead him away, a man appeared outta the mist, followed by a woman carryin a baby. All three of them was black folks.

The man stopped short when he seen us and the woman bumped into his back. I rememba her eyes was wild in her head and they was both breathin real hard.

"I seen you last night," I said fore the man could speak, "rowin cross the river. We is headin for Ohio, too, and my pa is right sick. We gotta cross with you."

The man was very dark and his face was drawn up into a scowl that woulda shamed Henry Sewell, Masta Harris's overseer. I think he mos likely wanted to give me a good thrashin, but there weren't no time cause them dogs was closin in fast. He leaned down over my pa for a moment, then hauled him up and laid him in the back of the boat, and he didn't speak nary a word while he went bout it. Then he ran to the front of the boat and yanked it toward the river like it didn't weigh no more than a butterfly. When he got the nose in the water, he stopped long enough for me and the woman to climb in fore he slid the boat into the river and jumped in himself. A second later, he was pullin on them oars like the devil himself was breathin down his neck.

And them dogs? When they come outta the fog, they mighta well been devils. They was barkin now, and growlin, and two of em jumped in the river and come swimmin after us. We wasn't more than twenty feet off, but them dogs wasn't no match for the man yankin them oars. He headed straight out and we crossed from the fog into the moonlight with the dogs fallin more and more behind.

Fore I could even think that we done escaped, three mens come runnin up to the banks of the river. All three was carryin rifles and they didn't hesitate. They raised up them guns and commenced to shootin.

"Git down in the boat," the man said. But I was already divin down on top of Pa, and the woman with her baby was rollin up next to us. I couldn't see nothin from where I was, but I could hear well enough. I could hear the crack of the bullets and the whizzin sound they made passin through the air, and a thump when a bullet hit the boat. And I could hear the oars in the water, steady and strong. I knowed the man pullin them oars wasn't huddled safe in the bottom of the boat. He was riskin his life to git us across.

The shootin stopped when we was in the middle of the river and I picked up my head. The man was still pullin at the oars, steady and hard, but one side of his face was washed over with a liquid that looked black in the moonlight but that I knew was blood.

"Git down, girl. We ain't clear yet."

Real quick, I looked back the way we come and saw another boat on the river, a boat showin a lantern light in front. The next second, tongues of flame come leapin out toward us. I knowed they was guns fore I heard the sound of the bullets and I jumped back down, holdin to my pa with all my might. Pa was shakin bad and he sounded like he was tryin to breathe through water. His body was almos too hot to touch.

I can't rightly say how long it took us to cross that river. Longer than forever is the way I remembas. But the mist on the far side finally did swallow us up and the firin stopped. I started thinkin I was home free. Then Pa started to speak.

"Golden Lea, you there?" His voice was weak, a whisper, and iffen I wasn't right near him, I don't think I woulda heard him.

"I'm here, Pa."

"You tell em, girl."

"Tell em what?"

Pa didn't say nothin more right then, jus held his peace so long I thought his words was comin from his fever. But he was only gatherin his strength.

"You tell em, girl." This time he managed to grab hold of my hand.

"You ain't makin sense, Pa. Tell em what?"

His hand tightened hard round mine. "You tell em Elijah Jackson died a free man."

I grabbed my pa and hung on to him till the boat finally turned into the bank. Things happened fast after that. The man rowin the boat mighta been shot, but he knew right well what woulda happen to him iffen he got caught. He leaned down into the boat and touched me, then my pa. When he spoke, his voice was firm, but not unkind.

"Your pa's done passed over."

The pain cut right down to my heart till there weren't nothin but the pain. There weren't no more river, no more slavery, no more fog and night. I felt a darkness risin up to close off my mind. I couldn't think and I didn't want to think. I didn't even want to find my way out.

"You gotta go."

I barely heard him and I figure now that he understood what I was goin through. He didn't try to convince me of nothin, jus grabbed hold of my arms and pulled me off.

"I can't leave my pa here," I shouted. "I can't leave him like this. Oh, please, Lord, please. At least let me bury my pa."

The man didn't answer, maybe rightly since I really weren't talkin to him anyway. He carried me, with the woman and the baby in tow, along a narrow path to a road that weren't more than a pair of ruts. There was a wagon pulled by a mule standin there and the man climbed onto the back of the wagon without lettin go of me. He crawled down under a canvas and the wagon started off, leavin Pa further and further behind.

I been in darkness, fore and since. When I lost my youngest daughter, Iris, seven years ago, my heart near split in half. But that didn't come close to what happened to me when Pa died. Fact, I couldn't even think that thought—that my pa was dead. No, better I shouldn't think at all. I shut myself down the minute I was pulled outta that boat.

We was taken to a cabin way up in the woods that first night. What I rememba bes is the two black mens who stood on a little porch. They was holdin muskets cross their chests and it was the first time I seen black mens take arms and ready to defend themselfs. They didn't say nothin as we passed into the house, didn't even look in our direction. Their eyes was fixed on the road.

Inside the house, a man and a woman, both white folks, stood ready to meet us. The woman tole us her name and bout how she was gonna help us till we come further north. She said the danger weren't over, not yet. The peoples livin in this part of Ohio didn't have no love for escaped slaves.

She went on for a time after that, but I can't recall nary a word. Can't rememba her name or even what she looked like. There was food, but I couldn't eat a crumb, and my sleep was no more restful than iffen I stayed awake through the night. And I didn't speak, neither, even when the woman knelt beside me and took my hand. She was right kindly, but her words didn't have no more meanin than the buzzin of bees.

We set off the next night, hid in the false bottom of a wagon bearin all manner of goods. This was a travelin tinker's wagon that stopped at the little farms, sellin everythin from pots and needles to remedies. The woman with the baby—her name was Mary—was right scared to crawl into that dark space every mornin. But I was glad for the dark, like I was glad for the steady pull of the mules and the turnin of the wheels and the creak of the wagon bed. Lost in the sounds, I shrank down. I became smaller and smaller and smaller.

After a time—some days, I think, but maybe a week—we come to a town in the state of Pennsylvania where I stayed for a spell at a farmhouse. The house was owned by a white couple name of Augustin. I weren't eatin hardly nothin and I weren't talkin cept to say yes or no. The Augustins tried to cheer me, but it weren't no use and it got to the point where they didn't *knowed what to do with me. That's when they decided to hand me over to Harriet Keaveny.*

Thinkin back, I gotta admit that Harriet saved my life. That don't mean she was some kinda angel of mercy. No, sir. Harriet was the mos no-nonsense woman I ever come across. Maybe that's on accounta she was born free, a black woman who never lived as a slave. She was tall, too, taller than mos mens, and built big.

"Girl," she said the first time she laid eyes on me, "I am a midwife by trade and I'll be teachin you to be my apprentice."

My own opinion weren't asked for. No, without another word bein spoke, my things was packed up and I was took away to a small house on State Street. And Harriet didn't waste no time when we got there. She led me into a room in the back and closed the door behind us. There was a rugged cross on the wall, rough-chopped outta hickory, and a small table beneath the cross. Flowers was set on the table.

"Golden Lea, it's time you prayed for your daddy's soul," she said. "You won't never find no peace of mind till you do. Tell me y'all daddy's name."

I was so surprised I answered without thinkin. "Elijah," I said.

And that was that. Harriet started into prayin, callin my pa's name while she rocked back and forth. She tole him he could rest easy, that his daughter was in good hands now, a free woman. She tole him that we was in a town called Eerie, which is only a short ways from Canada, so that even iffen the slave catchers was to come for me, I would find me a safe place at hand. She tole him she would make me into a healer and give me the power to bring new life into this world and that I would go on to have chirrens of my own.

Then she prayed directly to the Lord. She said we wasn't none of us perfect, not even the most humble among us, and that Elijah was a sinner, too. She knowed that but she begged that he find a place fore the throne, a simple man who done his bes.

Harriet stopped there and looked direct at me, waitin. And somethin come to me, then—a truth, a rule for livin life that I carries to this very day. The Lord wants us to love and respect Him, and by doing so love each other—black, white, or brown—as we want to be loved. That much is everywhere to be found in the Bible, and I have tried to live my life by that rule to this very day.

But the Good Book don't no place say that the Lord is one bit interested in our approval. He got His ways and we mortals gotta live on, no matter how bad our hurts.

I didn't pray, not that afternoon. I tole my story to Harriet instead, tole bout my mama bein sold off and how the thought of spendin the rest of my life as the slave of a treacherous girl like Missy Ann caused me to yearn for my freedom. I tole her that my pa was my only comfort and that Masta Harris was gonna sell him off. I tole her how we come through the forest and what we seen on our way, bout Jack Trembley and Cloud Dreamer and ol Silas. And I tole her Pa's last words to me as he lay dyin.

"Tell em Elijah Jackson died a free man."

Then I cried till there wasn't no more tears in my body. I cried till the poison in my mind flowed out with my tears.

That very night, Harriet took me to the home of an escaped slave name of Evvie Green and I watched a new baby come into the world for the first time. I seen what a struggle it was and how the child was completely helpless and I knowed right then that I was also helpless. And jus like that boy child had to look to his mama to survive, I had to look to the Lord. There weren't nothin else to it, no way to git round the fact. The Lord was my shepherd, whether I liked it or not.

I seen a lot and been through much since the day Harriet Keaveny took me in. I found me a husband, a good man— Mista Amos Pitts, and we had four chirrens who give me a passel of grand-chirrens. I lived through the big war between the states, too—the Civil War—and went along to the battlefields with the 54th Regiment, which was composed of black soldiers. I seen a hundred and sixteen of those black mens killed in a day at Fort Wagner, and as many more carried off the field with terrible wounds. I knows cause I prayed over every one.

I thought that war was never gonna end, that blood was destined to flow forever. But it finally did end and I went back north. Lands, you'd think I woulda stayed put for a spell, but only a coupla years later, I was off again, to look for my mama.

But the closest I ever got to my mama was a slave buryin ground in Alabama. There weren't no markers or nothin. Slaves wasn't figured to be worth remembrin and I wasn't even sure my mama was lyin in that field. But I fell to my knees anyway, and I cried and I prayed. I cried and prayed for my mama and my pa and for all them that lived and died in slavery. I prayed the Lord would take them into His heart. Sadly, I never found a trace of my mama, jus have my mind's images of her in a long line of slaves covered in white dust and the clank, clank, clank of the chains hittin against the rocks.

All that was a long time ago and it wears me some even to think on it. I'm a ol woman now, and writin this much has mos near sucked out what little energy I got left. Sides, Christmas is comin soon and I mean to knit sweaters and socks for the grand-chirrens. Times is still hard for black folks and the days is turnin colder.

I been neglectin my Bible, too, and I feel a need to take it up again. Gittin older is also gittin closer, iffen you takes my meanin. So, come the mornin, I'm jus gonna hand this writin to Ophelia and hope it's to her satisfaction, and pray that these recollections will provide some whisper of hope to her chirrens and their'n.

This here I can say for sure. I tole my story as true as I can recollect it and I didn't leave nothin out—not the good nor the bad.

—Golden Lea Jackson Pitts
November 1898

Chapter 14

LOST AND FOUND

COMING HOME WAS weird. It was like I'd never been there before, like I was seeing my own home for the first time. I remember leaving the hospital that day, as scared of walking out as I had first been of walking in. It's not that I loved it there by any stretch of the imagination. It wasn't exactly a four-star hotel. But I'd been cared for there. And I had come through some hard times there. And, in a way, I grew up there.

Then I started getting used to being back home again. I e-mailed the Mag-7s to let them know I was okay. It was my first step toward reaching out to my "old" life again.

I got comfortable snuggling beneath my down-alternative blanket pretty quickly, though it took me a while to fall asleep in the silence of my room, without all the blipping and beeping I had heard going on in the hospital. Who knew I'd miss something like that? The hospital food, however, not so much.

I did get into a bad habit of leaving the television on almost continuously. It had been my constant companion/diversion in the hospital room, and it would take me a while to break that one, much to Mom's displeasure.

Of course, before I could really readjust to being home, the whirlwind started all over again. First, the relatives began to show up—aunts, uncles, grandparents, even a few cousins. The trips to our house were a kind of pilgrimage, and I guess that made me the shrine. But I was touched, even when I was treated like a wilting flower expected to die at any minute. That was something Mom and Dad had stopped doing. They saw the way I fought and knew I wasn't fragile.

But, despite them wanting to spoil me, the best part about my relatives is that not one of them cared how I looked. Sure, I got some sympathetic glances thrown my way when they first saw me, and my grandmothers were in a kind of competition to see who could fatten me up the fastest. But they all hugged me, and kissed me, and stroked what was left of my hair without once flinching. No one was disgusted to be near me or worried they'd catch what I had. Like I said: Family, you gotta love them.

Then, just as soon as I got used to the constant flurry of having the extended family in our house, the relatives had to leave and resume their normal lives. They were hardly even gone when I had to resume mine—in the form of radiation therapy.

My first chemo treatment came a week after that. Talk about sick. I didn't know the true depth and nuance of the word "nauseous" before that. I was so sick to my stomach all the time that I dug a well-worn groove in the carpet between the dining room table and the bathroom. Not to mention that there's nothing quite like staring down at a shower drain clogged by a pile of your own hair.

But even with all these treatments/various forms of torture, I never felt as bad as I did when my infection was at its worst—I never felt close to death again. And for that, I was thankful. But the treatments would continue for more than a year and I would be weak, nauseated, and bald for the duration. Talk about an unflattering Facebook picture!

But no matter how bad I felt, even on my worst days, I couldn't shake the urge to put it all down, if not on paper, at least on my computer screen. I'd wanted to be a writer for a long time, and reading Golden Lea's book did nothing to quell the urge. I'm not saying I had an *omigosh* moment. But I couldn't shake this little voice that kept telling me to get started. Although I did manage to ignore it for a few weeks. What can I say? I was living up to my full potential of laziness.

Beginning a few weeks after I got home, Josh Grappinelli and I began to schedule our treatments for the same time whenever possible. We'd e-mail or text each other to make sure we could each manipulate a parent into bringing us to the hospital at our chosen time. Usually, it worked. I mean, we weren't asking to go to Disneyland or anything like that!

I was always so happy to see Josh. No matter how worn down he looked, his spirits were always up, and that never failed to bring out the optimist in me, too. I never quite got around to telling him this, but under different circumstances, I would have definitely invited him to my next school dance. I mean, Jason Walker was cute. But what does, like, hair have to do with anything? Josh was amazing. *And* he was from Brooklyn. *And* he helped me discover the first real "work" that I believe I was meant to do.

After our treatments, Josh and I visited patients in Samuelson Hospital's various units. Let me tell you, there's nothing like the sight of a two-year-old with cancer to cut through your own self-pity. The little kids all had this same bewildered look in their eyes, like they couldn't quite comprehend what was happening to them, and they tended to cling to things—a toy, a stuffed animal, a comic book. But, boy, were they always so happy to see us!

We read to them mostly, read to them and held their hands. Josh played video games with them, which was when the kid in him would come out, too. When the children got to know us better, they'd even let us play with their cherished toy, stuffed animal, or comic book with them. They'd share it with us for a few minutes, unafraid to let go. That's when I knew we had their trust—and that it was a special, sacred gift.

I remember one girl especially, Hailey Noel Reed. Hailey was three years old and her cancer had spread to her bones. She was no longer being treated for anything but pain, and her body was shrunken, her wrists as thin as broomsticks. But she was as courageous as any kid in the hospital. I would sit on the edge of the bed, laying the book down where we could both see it, and point to the pictures as I went along.

Hailey invariably fell asleep before I finished the book, her eyes fluttering for a moment before they closed. I'd sit next to her for a while, holding her hand while I watched her thin chest rise and fall. Hailey's blond hair was growing in. Maybe three inches long, it fanned out from her scalp like the halo of an angel.

It was easier with the older kids. They wanted to know what was going to happen next, what it would feel like, how we dealt with it. They reminded me most of myself. They asked the same questions that I had asked Dr. Balder when I first came in. And the simple fact that Josh and I had most of the answers—and looked like a couple of ghouls—only enhanced our prestige among them. Really, from the reaction we got, you'd think Miley Cyrus and one of the Jonas brothers had walked in, instead of two bald skeletons!

But if ghoul-dom was prestigious within the hallowed halls of Samuelson Hospital for Pediatric Neurology, it had just the opposite effect when I tried to resume my life as a suburban teenager in Montclair. I got stared at wherever I went. Which is not to say that I went out much, not in the beginning. For the first couple of weeks, I only left the house for treatments. It wasn't about vanity anymore. I was just that weak. And after the treatments, I felt too sick to attend school.

That's where Marsha the Nerd came in. I wanted to graduate middle school with my class and Principal Tuttleman agreed to let me, assuming I passed my final exams. I thought that shouldn't be too hard with Marsha as my tutor.

Some days it seemed like everything I did reminded me of Golden Lea. This was even true when Marsha came over. Golden Lea referred to Harriet Keaveny's no-nonsense attitude and her tough love approach to problems. Well,

Marsha the Nerd had a sharper tongue than any teacher I ever met, and she made no allowances for my weakened condition. Chemo was not an excuse, as far as Marsha was concerned. I was there to learn. She was there to teach. In fact, I was pretty sure she was going to add me to her eventual college applications: Tutored brain-damaged child. But only if I passed.

Over time, I came to realize that Marsha's tough-as-nails attitude was her way of dealing with my illness, not to mention my altered appearance. Marsha didn't care how people looked naturally: buck teeth, big ears, big deal! But this was not how I normally looked. It was a combination of chemicals and cancer, and seeing her best friend so ravaged and changed by illness scared her, I think. Maybe it made her feel vulnerable, or reminded her of our mortality. Either way, my drastically different appearance was something that Marsha, as open-minded as she was, was having a hard time wrapping her mind around.

And that's not to mention my other friends, who were *really* struggling with the situation. Jasmine the Bengali Rose, Ken the Karate Kid, and a few others from the Mag-7s did visit from time to time, but I could tell they weren't comfortable. And neither was I. Even though I knew better, I couldn't shake the feeling that they thought I was somehow contagious. Like if I got too close to them, they'd catch my bad luck. I know that wasn't really what they felt. In fact, what they were feeling was probably too complex to put into words. I mean, come on! We were fourteen years old. Not exactly experts at expressing our thoughts. But I do know that how they looked at me reminded me of how I looked at the young cancer patients in the waiting room when I first went to get my MRI. There was "us" and "them." In my friends' eyes, I wasn't part of "us" anymore.

I knew something had happened to me and that my life was changing. And while I wouldn't say the Mag-7s had become irrelevant, the divisions between some of us only grew wider over time. Guess it was bound to happen sooner or later during high school, anyway.

Not so with Marsha. After a single confrontation—which had nothing to do with my sickness, but was over a stupid algebra problem, of all things—we finally came to accept each other.

"Ya know, Nerd," I said, after she made a particularly sarcastic comment about my inability—or what she called my "unwillingness"—to catch up or to pay attention, "if I had the strength—which I will some day—I'd kick your obnoxious caboose from here to the top of First Mountain."

She looked at me for a minute, then said, "Am I really that bad?"

"Worse."

I expected an argument. Especially since Marsha was always up for a debate. But this time she just stared at me, her eyes, behind her cat-eye glasses, swollen and vaguely out of focus.

"Everything I do is designed to build a wall," she said. "I know I'm obnoxious. The sad fact is that I like being obnoxious. I think it's one of the ways I've learned to deal with…you know, my home life." She smiled. "Now I think I'm building a wall to distance myself from you."

"What?" I said. "You mean, like, a barrier to keep the leper away?"

"No," she said. "I mean like a protective wall to keep my feelings in check. I almost lost my best friend, you know. I think my obnoxiousness toward you is a defense mechanism so that I won't get hurt like that again."

I smiled. "First of all, I'm fine. You don't have to worry about losing me any time soon. Second of all, that's the sweetest thing I've ever heard from such an obnoxious person."

She shrugged. "Who knows? I may turn it into an asset. When I get into Harvard, I might even major in obnoxiousness."

"You should, since you're so good at it."

For Marsha the Nerd, this was as close to a boo-hoo moment as she got. I tried to remember the last time she'd actually apologized. For anything. I think it was after she beaned me with a Twinkie in the lunchroom when we were in the second grade. And even then, her parents made her apologize. I still think she was only sorry about having wasted a perfectly good Twinkie.

After that warm, fuzzy moment between Marsha and me, it all got better. I studied harder and she eased up on the sarcastic remarks. Call it a compromise. Plus, I stopped stressing over whether or not I'd pass my exams. I'd leave that to Marsha. In my opinion, there were bigger issues in life. According to her, though, I absolutely *had* to pass. If I didn't, the shame of my failure would force her to commit *hari-kari*. Great, now I was responsible for *her* survival.

Needless to say, my illness brought me closer to my parents. No doubt about it. They were there for me every step of the way, and they shared my pain, measure for measure. I couldn't have asked for anything more. Yet I got it anyway: Daddy stopped traveling so much and Mom started coming home for dinner every night, even when she had a major trial going on. I think my sickness made them realize what was important in life, too. Of course, none of us said that. We didn't need to. We just *knew* it.

And speaking of dinners, I started cooking again, partly because I could take my time and stop to rest as often as I needed. But mainly because it was something I could do for my parents to pay them back for all they'd done for me. Not that they'd ever ask. But Daddy wasn't exactly saying no to my home-cooked lasagna, which always came out better than my mother's failed attempts that looked more like a science-project-gone-bad. For the most part, I cooked healthy, but I broke out the cholesterol big time on special occasions, like Mom's birthday.

For that important family celebration, I spent most of the day preparing her favorite meal—smothered pork chops, fried cabbage, and dirty rice—stopping only to work on my upcoming science exam in the afternoon, and the effort yielded results. Mom started drooling before the door closed behind her, and dinner came off without a hitch.

I was really tired afterward, but I waited until she opened her presents and the candles were blown out on an ice cream cake before I left my father to load the dishwasher and headed upstairs.

For a short time, I lay on my bed and lost myself in an old rerun of *The Cosby Show* while I gathered my strength. I eventually clicked off the television and closed my eyes, thinking about all the big milestones my parents and I had marked together. All of our birthdays, and my grammar school graduation. Every New Year's Eve and their anniversaries, and whenever I got a particularly good report card. When I survived my first summer at sleep-away camp, and whenever Mom won any huge case that she had been working on for months. We were always there for each other every time it really counted, so I shouldn't have been surprised one bit that they were supporting me through each step of my recovery, just as they had through every second of my sickness.

I looked up at my multiracial Wall of Fame and stared at the various faces. I thought about all the milestones yet to come that we would hopefully have a chance to celebrate together. My high school and college graduations—that is, of course, if I could get through middle school with Marsha's help. The dinner at whatever restaurant I'd treat them to with my first real paycheck, doing something that I planned would make the world a better place. Marriage? Grandchildren? We'd see about that in the distant future.

Yes, I was getting better—despite the treatments, the hair loss, and the fatigue. My use of words continued to improve, though there were still times when I couldn't force a particular word past my lips. The curious part was that I could write the words I couldn't speak, a reality I became aware of when I began to send out e-mails shortly after I came home from the hospital. So what excuse did I have for not getting started on that book I said I'd write? True, I had difficulty concentrating for any length of time, but that was due to fatigue, not an attention-deficit disorder like Marsha sarcastically implied. I would just have to go slowly with that project, as I did when I prepared Mom's dinner.

Everything didn't exactly come up rosy, though, I realize. A brain tumor isn't quite a TV sitcom that could be cured and tied up in a neat little bow with a happy ending for everyone after only thirty minutes. Not even Dr. Huxtable could pull that one off. There were losses, too. First, I was still having some trouble with my balance. I could walk all right, and even run a little in a straight line, but sudden turns left me momentarily dizzy. My physical therapist informed me that this was a deficit that would probably improve somewhat over time, but never completely disappear.

That meant I would no longer be the Montclair Flash. Okay, so that in itself seems like NBD (no big deal, remember?). Like, I'll find another nickname, right? But it also meant that I would never be the basketball star I had once hoped to become. Basketball is all about quick, lateral movements—movements I couldn't now execute without falling flat on my face. I would never compete in the Olympics, or in the WNBA, or even in high school. And any kind of sports scholarship was out of the question. Those dreams were gone for good. Marsha was right. I would have to study math a little harder to get a free ride into Harvard now.

Second, besides the strained friendships I already mentioned, I lost some of my confidence about returning back to school. My grand reentrance would be at the FDR Middle School graduation, where I expected to be stared at like some sort of freak. Fortunately, everybody looks a little dorky in those square cardboard caps—plus the tassel will go a long way toward hiding my lack of hair. But the real challenge would come at the end of summer and the beginning of high school: ninth grade. I know that some kids will be cruel and others will just be curious. But I can't really say that I'm looking forward to my constant turn at show and tell. What makes it worse is that Marsha won't even be with me, since she's changing to her other school.

I keep telling myself that school is not a fashion show anyway, and I'll be there to focus on academics. But that won't stop the other students from pointing, or laughing, or looking away when they're talking to me. It's not that those reactions will wound me deeply. *Puh-leeeze*, I know better than that. It's more like I don't want to be disappointed in my classmates and feel uncomfortable in my surroundings.

Still, school's a good four months away and who knows? I may look pretty normal by that time. The thing is, I don't think I'll *feel* normal. Because the final thing I lost, for better or worse, is the simple ability to be a carefree kid. Things that everybody takes for granted? I don't anymore. I can't sweat the small details, and I won't waste time on anything that's unimportant to me. Who can afford to, after all? Who stole whose boyfriend, and will anyone ask me to the dance, and what are you wearing on Friday night are not serious life and death issues. Not that I think I'm *above* all the melodrama—which is, after all, half of the high school experience—or that I'm better than anyone else. Just that Josh was right: I can't go back to what I once considered "normal."

But whatever I lost, whatever my illness has taken away, there are gains, too. My faith in God is stronger—as is my faith in myself. Golden Lea's story of hope and perseverance has really inspired me, and I'm trying to live each day by her rule: Love God, and love others as you want to be loved.

And the plus side of no longer fitting into "normalcy" is that all of those small teenage fears that are blown up to larger-than-life proportions—fears enhanced by my multiracial status, my gawkiness, my insecurities—have simply vanished. Will I be popular, will I be able to afford the coolest gear, will I have a handsome boyfriend, or get into that top-tier college? Those problems have receded so far into the past that I barely recognize the girl who'd considered them the most important questions in life.

I just hope they're not replaced by a nagging worry that the brain tumor will reappear. So far, I haven't really allowed myself to dwell on that possibility. Like Josh said, who wants to live that way? Dr. Balder assured me that my type of tumor wasn't necessarily recurring, and the fact that it's slow-growing means that with continued monthly exams and some extra vigilance on my part, we can keep it under check. Since no one's given a guarantee in life, I'd say I'm happy to at least have good odds. Besides, as I'm constantly reminded whenever I look around me, I am pretty lucky.

Anyway, these are the types of thoughts that went round and round in my mind, until I finally hauled myself out of bed an hour later. I crossed the room to my desk, clicked on the lamp and turned on the computer. I opened Microsoft Word, and for a time, simply stared at the blank page on the monitor, the way I do at the beginning of a really big research paper. Then, for a few moments, I reflected on everything that had happened, from the day I collapsed on the basketball court to the present. I'd have to say it was quite a journey. Not one that I'd ever want to go on again, but one that I want to grow from.

Journeys, I had come to understand, were not always measured in miles, though that's how Golden Lea initially viewed hers. I knew that I could never go back to what I was. But the important thing is that I don't want to go back. I want to be who I am. And I look forward to who I will be after the many journeys ahead. I accept myself, as I am. All five-foot-ten of me.

I took a vow right then. Like my ancestor, Golden Lea, I vowed that I would tell my story as true as I could, and that I would leave nothing out—not the good nor the bad. Every single person's story is important and something can be learned from its telling—no matter how hard it is to relive, or how impossible it may be to find the right words.

Partly out of relief, and partly out of gratitude, I felt tears welling up in my eyes as I put my hands on the keyboard and began to type:

Coach Stover's face was as red as the Slimshine Urgent! lipstick that she wouldn't let me wear on the court. Intense? Major. And believe me, red was not her most flattering shade.

I mean, gimme a break. It wasn't like we were playing in the WNBA finals, or even the Olympics, which was my goal five years down the line. No, this was girls' basketball in suburban Montclair: Franklin D. Roosevelt Middle School against Benton Middle School....

www.ingramcontent.com/pod-product-compliance
Lightning Source LLC
Chambersburg PA
CBHW020514120726
47904CB00003B/822